ARCHETYPAL CHAKRAS

Meditations and Exercises for Opening Your Chakras

Arnold Bittlinger

WEISERBOOKS
Boston, MA/York Beach, ME

First published in 2001 by
Red Wheel/Weiser, LLC
P. O. Box 612
York Beach, ME 03910-0612
www.redwheelweiser.com

Translated by Christine M. Grimm

Library of Congress Cataloging-in-Publication Data

Bittlinger, Arnold.
    [Chakren Meditation. English]
    Archetypal chakras/Arnold Bittlinger; [translated by Christine Grimm].
        p. cm.
    Includes bibliographical references (p.) and index.
    ISBN 1-57863-210-2 (pbk : alk paper)
        1. Chakras—Miscellanea.

BF1442.C53 B5813 2001
    291.4'35—dc21   2001023387

Typeset in ACaslon

Illustrations: Copyright © 2001 Kösel-Verlag, Germany. Chakra symbols after
A. Avalon, *The Serpent Power*.

Printed in Canada

TCP

08 07 06 05 04 03 02 01
8 7 6 5 4 3 2 1

The paper used in this publication meets the minimum requirements of the American
National Standard for Information Sciences—Permanence of Paper for Printed Library
Materials Z39.48—1992 (R1997).

ARCHETYPAL CHAKRAS

Contents

List of Figures

List of Exercises
and Meditations

Introduction

An Indian yogi, Swami Amaldas, opened the door to the world of the chakras for me. C. G. Jung taught me to understand these ancient Indian chakra symbols. Consequently, this book begins with Jung's fundamental statements about the chakra system, which are the basis of my work. In the subsequent reflections on the individual chakra symbols, Jung's message is expanded and linked with practical experiences. I understand—as Jung did—the path of the chakras to be the path of self-actualization, and I see the individual chakra symbols as memory aids for the specific phases on this path of individuation. To help our understanding of the meaning of these phases, we will look at each chakra and practice a few simple physical exercises. When I was choosing these exercises, I wanted to make sure that each exercise expressed the significance of its respective chakra. I also felt it was important thatthe exercises be simple enough to be done easily by people who meditate. The exercises I found have become very dear to me as a preparation for the start of each new day.

In addition, I will also discuss the symbolic colors of the chakras and the personal chakra animals. Working with these chakra animals has proved to be a valuable aid in the therapeutic process.

The chapter titled "The Path of the Chakras in the Bible" ultimately demonstrates that the path of the chakras as a path to becoming whole corresponds to the inner structure of some well-known biblical texts. They also illustrate that the path of the chakras is a path of life for each of us, whether we come from Eastern or Western traditions.

Schaffhausen, Switzerland
—Dr. Arnold Bittlinger

Part I

The Chakras—
East and West

The Path of Individuation
and the Chakra Symbols

It happened at the C. G. Jung Institute in Zurich: I entered the office of the supervisor of studies for the first time and was completely surprised. All the walls in this office were decorated with large framed chakra symbols! They were copies of the pictures that Arthur Avalon (Sir John Woodroofe) published in his book *The Serpent Power* in 1918,[1] which are also reproduced in this book. And then I learned that long before the chakras became fashionable in the West, C. G. Jung had comprehensively studied these profound energy centers and provided helpful information about them.

It is also somewhat surprising that the chakra books filling the shelves of bookstores today rarely refer to Jung and his work. One possible reason for this may be the fact that the chakras are only mentioned in a few places within *The Collected Works of C. G. Jung*. On the other hand, he did speak extensively about the chakras in a number of seminars, but the transcriptions of these seminars have only been published to a limited extent.[2] I wrote this book to close this gap and explore what Jung has to say about the individual chakra symbols.[3]

For Jung, the chakra system reflects the process of individuation. What exactly is the process of "individuation"? What does Jung mean by this? He writes, "Individuation," in general, "is the process by which individual beings are formed and differentiated. . . . Individuation, therefore, is a process of *differentiation,* having for its goal the development of the individual personality."[4]

Marie-Louise von Franz compares this process with the growth of a mountain pine. She writes:

> One could picture this in the following way. The seed of a mountain pine contains the whole future tree in a latent form; but each seed falls at a certain time onto a particular place, in which there are a number of special factors, such as the quality of the soil and the stones, the slope of the land. . . . The latent totality of the pine in the seed reacts to these circumstances by avoiding the stones and inclining toward the sun. . . . Thus, an individual pine slowly comes into existence, constituting the fulfillment of its totality, its emergence into the realm of reality. Without the living tree, the image of the pine is only an abstract idea. Again, the realization of this uniqueness in the individual man is the goal of the process of individuation.[5]

Such a process can take its course unconsciously as a natural growth process—like it does in plants. However, this process only becomes the process of individuation in the actual sense of the word when the human being becomes conscious of this development.

> But [the human being] certainly is able to participate consciously in his development. He even feels that from time to time, by making free decisions, he can cooperate actively with it. This cooperation

belongs to the process of individuation in the nar-
rower sense of the word.[6]

Consequently, individuation means self-actualization
by becoming conscious. Jung says, "Individuation is practically the same as the development of consciousness out of
the original state of identity. It is thus an extension of the
sphere of consciousness, an enriching of conscious psychological life.[7]

The impulses for becoming conscious and also for self-
actualization do not come from the ego, but from the entirety of the psyche, the Self. Self-actualization, therefore,
means listening to what the inner wholeness, the self, wants
from me now in this situation, or wants to achieve through
me,[8] and then also listening to these impulses from the Self.

In this individuation process, we can distinguish between various phases or "manifestations," such as the identity phase, the first encounter with the unconscious, insight
into the shadow, withdrawal of projections, the encounter
with the anima or animus, and experiences with the Self.[9]

Jung recognized these manifestations of the psyche in
the illustrations from alchemy, astrology, the tarot, the
I Ching, and also those of the chakra system.[10] M. L. von
Franz writes in *Man & His Symbols*, "As it were, all religions
contain symbols that illustrate the individuation process or
important phases of it."[11] These also include the chakra
symbols with which we are concerned here. Jung considered
the chakra system to be among the "most outstanding Eastern examples" of a picture series to illustrate the symbolic
process."[12]

What is this chakras system? According to the teachings of Kundalini Yoga, each human being has a subtle
body that permeates and encircles the physical body. Life

energy flows through this subtle body. This energy is symbolically depicted as a snake, called *kundalini,* which lies rolled up at the bottom end of the spinal column and sleeps. (*Kundalini* means "the rolled-up one.")

On the path of meditation, it is important to awaken this kundalini and cause life energy to flow so that it can develop its healing power. According to the Indian mind-set the main channel of this energy flow runs along the spinal column. When energy rises through this channel, it distributes itself throughout the body, from the root chakra to all the other chakras up to the crown chakra. In visual terms, this stream of energy flows from "Earth" to "Heaven." The seven main chakras are located at the bottom of the spinal column, in the lower abdomen, solar plexus, heart area, throat, forehead, and at the top of the head. (See figure 1.)

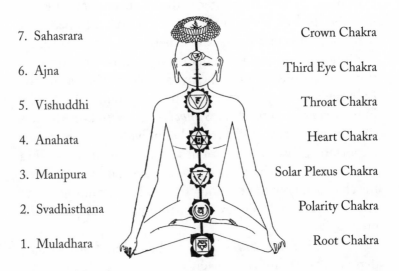

7. Sahasrara		Crown Chakra
6. Ajna		Third Eye Chakra
5. Vishuddhi		Throat Chakra
4. Anahata		Heart Chakra
3. Manipura		Solar Plexus Chakra
2. Svadhisthana		Polarity Chakra
1. Muladhara		Root Chakra

Figure 1.   The seven chakras.

The knowledge about the chakras is very ancient. It has been preserved and developed in India; however, the chakras are not "Indian" but human in general. That chakras are experienced and sensed in other cultures as well has been alluded to in some pictorial and architectural sources[13] as well as in Western texts where similar experiences have been described. According to Jung, we encounter the chakras not only in the teaching of yoga, but can also find similar concepts in old German alchemical works that would seem to have been created without any knowledge of yoga.[14] One example of this is the well-known *Chymische Hochzeit* ("The Chemical Wedding") by Valentin Andrae, which has been published in many forms.[15] The existence of the chakras can also be traced in other Western texts, such as some of the fairy tales. The Bible also contains texts that can be interpreted in the light of the chakra experience.[16]

Some people think that the chakras are the product of a rich imagination because they cannot be proved in the scientific sense. The question arises again: "Do chakras really exist?" On the one hand, Jung says that "these centers are merely metaphorical . . . but the Hindu, himself, says only that it is 'just as if' there were such centers."[17] On the other hand, ". . . the interesting thing is that the symptoms which occur when . . . the Kundalini mounts through these localized centers almost point to physiological facts; it is really 'just as if' there were centers like these which influence certain organs."[18] I want to leave this question open since we are considering the symbolic meaning of the chakras in this book, which is independent of the actual existence of such centers.

Jung calls the chakras a precisely developed system of "psychic layers, of localizations of consciousness up from the region of the perineum to the top of the head,"[19] or the flowerlike centers for various seats of consciousness."[20] Jung illustrates these facts with a picture.[21] This picture (see figure 2) shows a wheel-like circle. In its lower section, a woman on her knees and elbows is completely entangled in the roots. There are dark clouds below the circle. In the middle of the circle is a smaller circle in which a woman sits, holding a book in her hand. In the upper section, a woman stands with both arms stretching toward a circle of light. Jung writes that this picture depicts various phases of the individuation process.[22]

Figure 2.   The various phases of the process of individuation. (Plate 5 from Jung-Wilhelm, *The Secret of the Golden Flower*, London: Routledge, 1931).

In the lower part of the picture, the woman is caught in the chthonic wickerwork of roots (Muladhara in Kundalini Yoga). In the middle (which corresponds to the Anahata Chakra), the woman looks at a book. She educates her mind and increases her knowledge and consciousness. In *The Secret of the Golden Flower*, Jung mentions the middle picture, saying that the center art is a representation of contemplation.[23] "At the top [which equals Sahasrara], reborn [as Renata] she receives illumination in the figure of a heavenly sphere that widens and frees the personality, its round shape representing the mandala in its 'Kingdom of God' aspect, whereas the lower wheel-shaped mandala is chthonic. . . . Down below lurk unintegrated dark clouds. This picture demonstrates the not uncommon fact that the personality needs to be extended both upwards and downwards."[24]

When Jung asks about the meaning of the individual chakras, he does not merely accept the explanations in the Indian commentaries but interprets them on the basis of his own Western roots. He places great value on the following statement, "If we do not attempt to make the symbols of Tantric Yoga accessible to our Western minds and work with them, they will remain a foreign object in our system and prevent natural growth. Then the result will be second-hand growth or even poisoning."[25]

The Indologist J. W. Hauer also recognizes the justification for such a Western interpretation of the chakras. He believes that it is a legitimate approach to the chakras when we consider East Indian symbols from a Western perspective. In his opinion, the Western interpretations are just as correct as the East Indian: "I am not adverse to believing that when we search for the meaning of these symbols on our own, we will get just as close to their meaning as when we use the suggestions that appear here and there in Indian texts. Yes, we may be closer, or at least just as close, to the creative force of these symbols as the Indians who have written these commentaries. Consequently, we take the liberty of interpreting these symbols for ourselves."[26]

However, taking the path that the chakra symbols mark for us is even more important than interpreting and understanding them. Chakra symbols are the symbols of a path or process—namely, the individuation process. The point is not to just look at them or use them for meditation purposes, but also to live them: "The path of yoga only has a life-influencing meaning when it is seen as the other pole of concrete experience in life."[27] Hauer also quotes Buddha, who said that the pure meditative method does not lead into the depths but only to psychic states.[28] Hauer continues, "Looking at the chakras is only meaningful when the chakras are symbols of the real life that we have experienced and that has lived through us, which is then symbolically depicted and solidified in such a chakra."[29]

C. G. Jung has done us a great service by explaining how Westerners can understand and use the chakra symbols. He has shown a comprehensible way to access this wonderful system. The following pages will explain this in detail.

The Chakra Symbols in the Light of Analytical Psychology

In this section, we will discuss the chakras from the East Indian and Western psychological point of view. The original sources will be considered so you will be able to trace their origins and elements. This will be helpful in understanding the symbolism later on.

MULADHARA—ROOT (OR 1ST) CHAKRA

Muladhara (*mula* = root, *adhara* = center: root center) is the seat of kundalini. All forms of energy are contained within Muladhara, but they are not yet developed.

The element of the root chakra is earth.

For Jung, the root chakra is the world of consciousness in which everything unconscious is still slumbering. Muladhara is the starting basis for his approach to the path of individuation. "Muladhara is normal everyday life, the reality in which we live, our daily existence, our ordinary life. . . . We are connected with a certain place, the normal citizens of specific countries. . . . Interpreted psychologically, Muladhara is our consciousness. It is the place where the self and everything divine is asleep. . . . The Muladhara world is a totally banal place. There is the family, our work, theater, the train, or the bills that have to be paid."[1]

SVADHISTANA—POLARITY (OR 2ND) CHAKRA

Svadhistana (*sva* = what belongs to us, *sthan* = the place where we live: our own place where we live)

The element of the polarity chakra is water: "The water in Svadhistana is the water of baptism. . . . Baptism is a symbolic act of drowning. . . . The Makara can devour a person in the process. . . . But we can only be reborn through drowning. Today, instead of Makara, we say 'analysis' since analysis also means rebirth and the danger of drowning in the unconscious."[2]

This chakra symbolizes everything that also belongs to us—namely, the realm of the unconscious mind. The world of the unconscious is now added to the world of consciousness. Jung says, "The second center bears all the characteristics of the unconscious. The path out of Muladhara leads into the unconscious mind."[3] However, the unconscious mind behaves in a manner complementary to the conscious attitude so that a polarity is created between the conscious and the unconscious approach. "When we leave Muladhara and reach Svadhistana, the forces upon which we have previously leaned now attain a completely different weight. What carried us into the conscious world and held us there will become our worst enemy when we enter into the new world, the unconscious. . . . Whatever was a blessing on the earth will turn into an enemy in the unconscious mind."[4]

MANIPURA—SOLAR PLEXUS (OR 3RD) CHAKRA

Manipura (*mani* = jewel, *pura* = city: city of jewels)

The element of the solar plexus chakra is fire.

Jung suggests, "All emotional devils break loose in Manipura. After baptism, we go directly to Hell. Hell is the City of Jewels—a horrible paradox! But what is a person who doesn't stand in the fire? Where there is no fire, there is also no light. It is painful, it burns, it may even waste our time—but it is also a source of strength."[5]

> When you are in *Manipura*, you have no conflict, because you are the conflict itself, . . . you can be exploded into ten thousand pieces yet you are one with yourself, because there is no center from which to judge, there is nothing in between the pairs of opposites. For you are everything, you are also the pairs of opposites, you are this and that when you are emotional.[6]

Moreover, Jung has also said this of Manipura:

> The fire here . . . has a healing effect because the things which were separate and contradictory are fused together; it is a meeting fire, similar to the alchemical pot in which substances are mixed and melted together.[7]

This is the actual meaning of the Manipura chakra: What is separate becomes united. A *conjunctio oppositorum* occurs—the union of the opposites.

ANAHATA—HEART (OR 4TH) CHAKRA

Anahata (*an-ahata* = un-beaten)

The element of the heart is air.

Jung describes the difference between Manipura and Anahata in the following manner: "In Manipura, we have a pure emotional psychology—without any objectivity. We have no control over our own emotions—we are emotion. On the other hand, in Anahata we can say: 'I'm in a bad mood.' In Manipura, we are in such a bad mood that we can't even admit it. But a person in Anahata says, 'By Jove—you are right!' and that is the higher condition that is the difference between Manipura and Anahata."[8] Jung also says, "Out of this glowing center of passions, of emotions, from down in the solar plexus, something can rise into the kingdom of the air, into consciousness; it is a germ of higher consciousness which is contained originally in the fire below, but which can become airlike and mount to the head."[9]

Anahata is a state above the storm in the valley that corresponds with the *albedo* of alchemy. We can stand on the mountaintop and withdraw the projections and emotions that previously battered us and see them from a higher perspective—*au dessus de la melee*. The storm continues to rage, but we stand above it.[10]

However, Jung repeatedly emphasizes the danger of sinking from a "higher" to a "lower" state. He says that the Anahata region is the air region since it is the region of the heart and lungs, meaning of blood and air. Everything above the diaphragm is symbolized by a bird. The bird can mean thoughts or contents of the personality that belong to this higher level. When we descend to Manipura, the things of the higher level are destroyed or at least severely injured through the natural drives of the objects that are animated by our climbing down into the lower level. . . . People can live without injury in Manipura when they belong there—but everything that belongs in Anahata becomes injured in Manipura since we maintain the respectively lower state within us. In a certain sense, the mental condition of this lower state is within us, but it is under the control of the higher center in which we currently find ourselves. Consequently, when we are in Anahata, this center then rules all the centers below, but they continue to live. So when Anahata is injured or abolished, we don't suffer completely, we only suffer in as much as we are in *Anahata;* in as much as we are in Manipura, we do not suffer at all."[11]

VISHUDDHI—THROAT (OR 5TH) CHAKRA

> *Vishudda* = purity, *Vishuddhi* = cleansing. Both
> terms are used for this chakra; I prefer Vishuddhi.

The element of Vishuddhi is ether. Ether is the transition between matter and the spirit. C. G. Jung says, "Ether . . . is matter that is not matter, and that must necessarily be a concept."[12] Ether "elevates" matter.

To Jung, the world of the Vishuddhi chakra is the world of psychic reality: "The psychic experiences and not the data of earthly reality are what is real in Vishuddha. If, for example, we are forced to take action in an insurmountable way or prevented from it in the same manner,

we will feel the power of the elephant in Vishuddha."[13]
"This is the world where the psyche exists in itself, where
the phsychical reality is the only reality, or where matter is
only a thin skin round an enormous cosmos of psychical
realities."[14]

What does this mean? According to Jung, the psychic
facts have no relation to the material world. For example,
from the perspective of Vishuddi, the anger we may feel
about someone or something has nothing to do with this
person or this matter but is a phenomenon of its own. "I
am angry," for example, is purely subjective. The person
with whom I am annoyed may not even notice my anger
at all, which makes me even more angry. Neither the other
person—or the issue itself—annoys me; it is my own
shadow that annoys me. Jung says, "One should even
admit that all one's psychical facts have nothing to do with
material facts. . . . The anger you feel . . . is not caused by
. . . external things. . . . Your shadow appears in him.
. . . Your worst enemy is perhaps within yourself."[15] The
people we encounter in the outside world are exponents of
our own psychic state: "'I am always the same
Dr. Jung,' but the experiences that his analysands have
with him are extraordinarily different, which means that
they experience themselves in the encounter with the
analyst."[16]

The world of Vishuddhi is the world of symbols. We
always encounter ourselves in the symbol. When I encounter the darkness in a symbol, then I encounter the
darkness within myself. When I encounter the light in a
symbol, then I encounter the light within myself. When I
encounter the divine in a symbol, then I encounter the divine within myself.

AJNA—THIRD EYE (OR 6TH) CHAKRA

Ajna = instruction

Jung has written very little concerning the two highest chakras. He believes they lie in an area that no longer belongs to our commonplace level of experience, and that the energies of these chakras are also far from being attained by humanity as a whole.

In terms of the Ajna chakra, Jung says, "Here you know nothing but psyche. And yet, there is another psyche, a counterpart to your psychical reality, the non-ego reality, the thing that is not even to be called the self. . . . The psychical is no longer a content in us, but we become contents of it."[17]

Ajna means "instruction." The third eye is engaged in inner vision[18] and internal instruction. It is no longer associated with any kind of law, command, or regulation. Instead, this inner instruction is a force that causes something to happen.[19] "You are not ever dreaming of doing anything other than the force is demanding, and the force is not demanding it since you are already doing it, since you are the force."[20]

Ajna is human will becoming one with divine will. Jung also says that Ajna is the state of a total consciousness—not just self-consciousness but a consciousness that includes everything . . . every tree, rock, breath of air. You are all of this yourself. There is nothing that you are not. In such an endlessly wide consciousness, we also experience all the chakras at the same time, since this is the highest state of consciousness. And it would not be the highest state if it did not include all of the earlier experiences.[21]

SAHASRARA—CROWN (OR 7TH) CHAKRA

Sahasrara = Thousand-Leafed Lotus

Jung says that the Sahasrara Chakra is beyond any type of experience. In Sahasrara, there is only Brahman. There is no experience because it is one, without a second. It is the "not-two" and everything that is not two, which does not participate in the polarity, cannot be experienced.[22] This combination of "being" and "not being" is not possible in this world. Existence that is simultaneously nonexistence is called Nirvana.

What is Nirvana? When Buddha was asked whether Nirvana exists, he gave no response. When he was asked if there was no Nirvana, he also gave no response. In doing so, Buddha wanted to express that every statement about Nirvana is wrong because a statement presumes duality. By giving a name to something, I differentiate it from something else. Nirvana is everything and nothing. So our only choice is to be silent about it.

In summary, Jung also said that the chakras are intuitions about the psyche as a whole, about their various states and possibilities. They symbolize the psyche from a cosmic perspective; it is as if a super-consciousness, an all-encompassing divine consciousness, were to survey the psyche from above.[23]

So much for C. G. Jung's statements on the chakras. In all of the "steps" and "phases," we should keep in mind that the path of the chakras, just like the path of individuation, does not mean rising up into the "higher spheres." To the contrary, it is important that we remain firmly anchored in the root chakra whenever we "rise up." Something of the step we have reached will always be with us,[24] and this attained step must be practiced again and again.

M. L. von Franz says of this process: "How many times in analysis has one got a little bit out of the problem, really overcome a problem to a certain extent feelng at peace and to some extent at one with oneself so that the worst seems to be over?—but three weeks later it all begins again as if one had done nothing at all. Many repetitions are required before the experience is consolidated, until finally the work holds."[25]

Part II

The Chakras—Definitions

The Chakra Symbols and the Path of the Chakras

The symbol of the chakra path is the kundalini snake, which slumbers in the motherly primal origins of Earth and—once awakened—rises up through the individual chakras. It connects them with each other, filling them with psychic energy. However, the root chakra still continues to be the basis or the foundation of kundalini energy. Through kundalini, all the chakras receive a portion of the root chakra's power, remaining connected with Mother Earth as a result. The path of kundalini from the root to the crown chakra, therefore, means the union of Earth with Sky—the "mother" with the "father."

In mythology, the kundalini path is described as the uniting of Shakti and Shiva. Shakti is feminine kundalini energy. She has her center in the root chakra and rises from there. Shiva, who has his center in the crown chakra, meets her and accompanies her through the individual chakras. Even in the root chakra, Shiva and Shakti are shown together as the unification of Earth energy with Heaven energy. (See figure 3, page 24.)

THE CHAKRAS AND THE KUNDALINI PATH

The path of kundalini from the root to the crown chakra has intermediate stages, namely the five middle chakras

Figure 3.   A symbolic representation of meditating with kundalini energy. The meditator sits on the energy, but notice the protective "hood" at his head, above the crown chakra.

from the polarity chakra to the third eye. Kundalini connects the experiences of these intermediate stages with the root and crown chakras. As a result, when kundalini arrives at the crown chakra, it has seven heads, expressing the experience of the individual chakras on the path from the root chakra to the crown chakra. Consequently, this seven-headed apex of kundalini symbolizes the whole of its path ("the path is the goal").

THE CHAKRAS

The chakras are the body's own innate memory aids for the path of individuation. This is very significant. Our body constantly reminds us of the developmental processes within our soul. By directing our attention to each individual chakra, we experience them as reminders for stages in the individuation process.

There are an infinite number of chakras. The highest number that I have heard is 88,000. However, when the seven main chakras begin to move, all the other chakras move with them. The energy that is absorbed from the cosmos or the surrounding world through the chakras is called *prana*. The channels through which prana flows are called *nadi*.

People who can see chakras say they appear as blood-like structures[1] that turn like funnels as they suck in energy. This absorbed energy flows into the body and animates it. However, it is important that we do not soak up everything that surrounds us.

There are situations and places in which the atmosphere is not good. Then we must protect ourselves. This normally occurs automatically since the chakras are like flowers: they close when it is cold, and open when it is warm. Flowers absorb the sunlight and protect themselves against the cold. In a similar manner, chakras take in beneficial energy and protect themselves against harmful energy. However, many people have blocked chakras since the proper treatment of the chakras has been largely forgotten. Our chakras are either too open and absorb everything—including negative energy—or they are closed and don't let anything in—not even positive energy.

Through chakra meditation, we can once again learn the proper approach to the chakras. Then they can become flexible again. However, remember that the chakras are wide open after meditation. Before we return to everyday life, it is important to harmonize the chakras. There are various methods we can use to accomplish this.

Harmonizing the Chakras—The Stroking Exercise

Do this exercise while standing. First hold both hands on top of each other in the stomach area without letting them touch the body. Then keep them on top of each other and move them up the body until they are above the head, continuing to move them down to the nape of the neck. Once there, separate the hands from each other, and return to the starting position. Repeat this stroking motion about 10 to 12 times. You can also do this exercise in your imagination.

You can use this exercise when you are away from home and feel the need to set boundaries against negative influences. Once they have been harmonized, the chakras will "function" properly again, so that they only absorb positive energies and close themselves to negative energies.

Harmonizing the Chakras—The Sign of the Cross

The sign of the cross also has a harmonizing effect on the chakras. With your hand, form the longitudinal beam of the cross by moving it down from your head to the root chakra. Keep it close to your body. Form the crossbeam by moving your hand from one shoulder to the other. To do this, you can either move from right to left (as in the Orthodox tradition) or from left to right (as in the Catholic tradition). While you do this, you can speak these words: "Yours is the kingdom [head] and the power [root chakra] and the glory [one shoulder] forever and ever [other shoulder]. Amen." You can place your hand on your heart when you say Amen.

Harmonizing the Chakras— The Lemniscate (Infinity Sign)

Place your right hand on your solar plexus (below the navel; the distance from the body or clothing is approximately 2 inches). Slowly and gently move your hand to the right shoulder. Then move it above your head to the left shoulder, and then across the solar plexus to the right hip. Next, move it in a soft arc to the left hip and back to the solar plexus. You can repeat this exercise a number of times.

When you do it with the left hand, first move your hand from the solar plexus to the left shoulder, then over the top of the head to the left hip, and in a soft arc to the right hip, and back to the solar plexus. You can also place both hands on top of each other and do the exercise in both directions like this (the lemniscate formed by both hands has an especially strong harmonizing and protective effect). (See figure 4, page 28.)

THE PETALS

When we look at the chakra symbols, the varying number of petals is the first thing that catches our attention. In the symbol of the root chakra, we encounter four lotus petals; the next chakra has six. The solar plexus chakra has ten petals, and the next chakra has twelve. So the root chakra and the polarity chakra are differentiated by two petals, as are the solar plexus chakra and the heart chakra. On the other hand, there is a difference of four petals between the polarity chakra and the solar plexus chakra, and between the heart chakra and the throat chakra. The chakras that are only separated from each other by two petals have an especially close relationship.

The cross sum of the number of the two lower petals is 1 (4 + 6 = 10 = 1). The number 1 is the number of the root chakra. The root chakra is therefore the dominating one. It is activated, and finds its completion, in the polarity chakra.

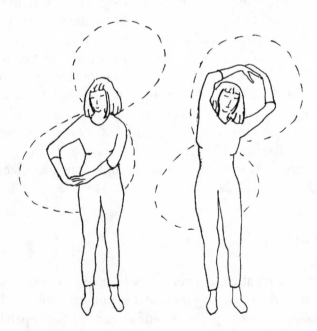

Figure 4. Making a figure 8 (lemniscate).

The third and fourth chakras also belong together. The cross sum here is 4 (10 + 12 = 22 / 2 + 2 = 4). The number four belongs to the heart chakra. So the heart chakra dominates here. The solar plexus chakra is oriented toward the heart chakra. The heart chakra is the developmental goal of the solar plexus chakra.

The sixteen petals in the fifth chakra result in a cross sum of 7. This chakra is a unity within itself. The sixth chakra, as the unification of masculine and feminine, is also a unity within itself.

In the uppermost chakra, the thousand-leafed lotus once again symbolizes the number 1. However, this 1 is no longer the undifferentiated 1 of the root chakra, but the differentiated unity of the entire chakra path in the crown chakra.

The Root Chakra—
Muladhara (1st Chakra)

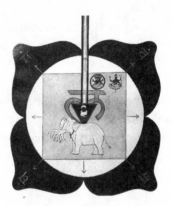

Figure 5.   The symbol of the root chakra.

The symbol of the root chakra has four petals. There is a Sanskrit letter in each of the petals. These are the last four letters of the Sanskrit alphabet. The Sanskrit alphabet has fifty letters, which are drawn on the petals from the root chakra to the third eye in a backward direction, from the last to the first letter.

At the center of the root chakra symbol is the sign LA, which stands for "earth." The circle above the letter is the sign of OM. OM is the all-encompassing letter. LA together with OM is spoken as "LAM." When we explore Sanskrit, we are on our very own soil because Sanskrit is an Indo-European language. Almost all of the European languages have their roots in Sanskrit.

Shiva is in the OM circle, with Shakti to his right.

The number 4 is strongly emphasized in the root chakra: four petals with four letters, the square with four sides, and the four corners all symbolize the earthly totality (the square only appears in the root chakra picture). This number is also repeated in the arrows, four of which are in the petals, and four are in the circle (the upper arrow is in the nadi), as well as the four legs of the elephant. The 4 reminds us of the four directions, the four seasons, the four elements, and four temperaments of our psyche (as well as their various developments, up to the 4 × 4 of the Jungian function types).

The square is integrated into a circle. This means that the earthly totality is integrated into the all-inclusive heavenly totality.

According to Linda Fierz and Toni Wolffe, C. G. Jung writes the following about the root chakra.

> Muladhara, as our root, is—interpreted psychologically—our consciousness. It is the place where the self and everything divine slumbers. The earth is our root. Here we stand firm. When we look around, we orient ourselves according to the four directions quite involuntarily because our location is the mandala of the earth. Everything that we can say about the Muladhara also applies to our world, to this dark place of unconsciousness where we are victims of circumstances and can achieve very little through our reason. . . . Here we are exactly like all the other people, caught in the *participation mystique* and guided by impulses and blind instincts. Only on Sunday morning when we go to church, or out into nature, are we perhaps overcome by a premonition of the next chakra. This

Sleeping Beauty—the self, the non-ego—wakes up
and moves a bit; then we wish that we could do
something somewhat unusual. But the Muladhara
world, where we are just as reasonable or unreason-
able as animals, is a very banal place.[1]

The animal in Muladhara is the elephant, which stands
firmly with four legs on the earth. The seven trunks make it
clear that this chakra contains all seven chakras. The entire
ascent is potentially already contained within the root
chakra. The two sets of four arrows are symbols for the energy of the kundalini.

At the center of the chakra, we see a "feminine" triangle
(yoni) that points downward. This triangle contains a masculine symbol (lingam) around which the kundalini is
wound three-and-a-half times. The white cap at the upper
end of the lingam already alludes to the crown chakra,
meaning that the entire path of the kundalini is already potentially contained within the root chakra.

THE WORLD OF CONSCIOUSNESS

The root chakra is the seat of the kundalini snake, where
all of the energies are contained but not yet developed. All
of the unconscious elements are still slumbering. Living in
the root chakra means living in the here and now, taking
everyday life seriously. The root chakra is the starting point
for every chakra meditation. It is the reality in which we
live. Living in the root chakra means fulfilling the task for
which we are on Earth, in the place where we have been
put where we stand firmly on the ground like the elephant,
bearing the burdens of everyday life. Moreover, the elephant is the "symbol of the domesticated libido, which

could be approximately equated with the horse in our own symbolism. It means the willpower or drive to act in a conscious manner."[2]

So what does it mean when we approach the world of consciousness in the root chakra? Marie-Louise von Franz compares the psyche with a sphere.[3]

In figure 6, consciousness (A) is the illuminated portion of this sphere. It appears to be lit by a spotlight. The center of consciousness is the ego. The Self is at the center of the overall personality, which includes the unconscious area (B) and the conscious area (A). Expressed in biblical terms, we could say that the Self is the "Christ within us." In self-actualization, the ego is increasingly directed by the "Self," until it ultimately merges with the Self in the Ajna chakra (the third eye). The process of becoming conscious means stimulating the ego-Self axis. The Self is then able to exercise more influence on the ego.

We can also clearly depict the conscious and unconscious reality in figure 7 on page 34.

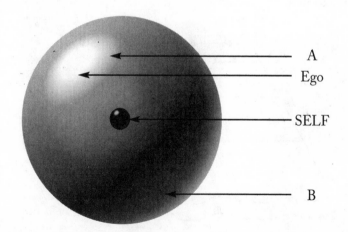

Figure 6.   Consciousness in the root chakra.

In the root chakra, we are only dealing with conscious reality. This is represented in the tip of the triangle because we first encounter the world of the unconscious in the polarity chakra.

As long as we "just" live in the world of consciousness, we are living "unconsciously." This means that we are not aware of the essential areas of our psyche and these occasionally disturb our superficial level of life through all types of Freudian slips, blunders, and the like.[4]

PSYCHOLOGICAL TYPES

In outer reality (the root chakra), we each function in our own way. The idea that we are all different was already obvious in antiquity. Even back then, people were seen as belonging to four different types. (See figure 8, page 35.)

C. G. Jung has changed this scheme because of his own exploration of the psyche. Figure 9, page 35, shows his breakdown.

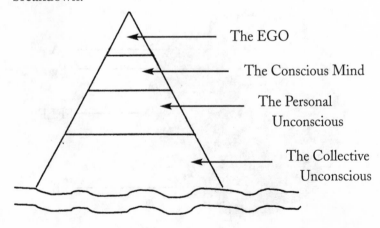

Figure 7. The layers of reality.

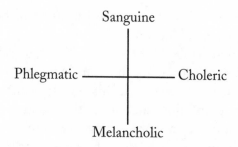

Figure 8.   The four basic psychological types.

Furthermore, Jung additionally differentiates between the extroverted (oriented toward the outside world) and introverted (oriented toward the inside world) types.[5]

For Jung, the thinking function and the feeling function are "judging" functions. The thinking type judges according to, "What is right? What is wrong?" The feeling type judges according to, "What is pleasant? What is unpleasant?" The other two functions do not judge, but simply perceive what is there. The sensation type perceives the outer reality; the

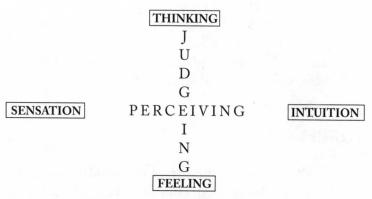

Figure 9.   Jung's psychological types.

intuitive perceives the inner. As the archetype of the human being, Jesus unites all four types.[6]

In the first half of life, one function generally rules. Jung calls this the "dominant function." Human beings first learn to assert themseves with this specific function. Jung gives the name "inferior function" to the function opposing the dominant function. For example, feeling is the inferior function for thinking types. Pure thinking types have a very hard time accessing their feelings, and pure feeling types have problems with logical thought. (The second half of life focuses on integrating the neglected function.)

The thinking type considers the intuition and sensation to be auxiliary functions. These can be used to gain access to the inferior function. Since a person is also extroverted or introverted, with the addition of the dominant function and auxiliary functions, there are sixteen type possibilities in the Jungian-type scheme. For example, an extroverted thinking type could have intuition as an auxiliary function.[7]

The way that the various functions flow into each other can best be expressed through the yin/yang symbol, for the light area is the conscious area, the dark is the unconscious. (See figure 10, page 37.)

In addition to the Jungian function types, there are other type models including the enneagram that readers could explore.[8] For many people, the personal cosmogram (or astrological birth chart) is especially helpful.[9]

THE PERSONA

The so-called persona is also part of the world of consciousness. C. G. Jung has defined it like this: "The persona is . . . a functional complex that comes into existence for reasons of

THINKING

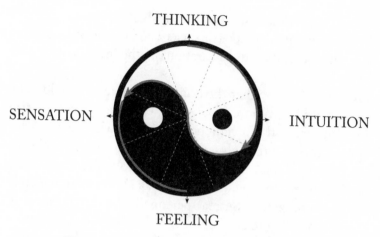

SENSATION   INTUITION

FEELING

Figure 10.   The tao and the Jungian types.

adaptation or convenience, but is by no means identical with individuality."[10] To a certain degree, the persona means a splitting of the personality. Jung says in CW 6:

"Angel abroad, devil at home," is formulation of the phenomenon of the character-splitting personality derived from everyday experience. A particular milieu necessitates a particular *attitude*. The longer this attitude lasts, and the more often it is required, the more habitual it becomes. Very many people from the educated classes have to move in two totally different milieus—in the domestic circle and the world of affairs. These two totally different environments demand two totally different attitudes, which, depending on the degree of the ego's *identification* with the attitude of the moment, produce a duplication of character. In accordance with the social conditions and requirements, the social

character is oriented on the one hand by the expec-
tations and demands of society, and on the other by
the social alms and aspirations of the individual.[11]

He goes on to say that the domestic character should generally be shaped more in keeping with the subject's desire
for comfort and convenience, which is why people who
appear to be extremely energetic, courageous, stubborn,
strong-willed, and inconsiderate in public life are seen as
good-natured, soft, yielding, and weak at home. So which is
the true character, the real personality? This question is
often impossible to answer.

With a persona, I show myself to others as I would like
to be seen. It is advantageous for me, according to my experience, as well as being a way to draw as little attention to
myself as possible.

Two extremes should be avoided in the development of
the persona. On the one hand, rejecting the persona and behaving in an egotistical manner on every occasion without
any consideration of the surrounding world; on the other
hand, totally identifying with the persona ("mask").[12]

C. G. Jung published[13] a picture by a woman that shows
her in the root-chakra phase. (See figure 11, page 39.) This
woman feels herself to be pure and unblemished, but far
below is the suppressed shadow area. This is typical for the
Muladhara situation in which the unconscious still slumbers
and the human being lives in the illusion of being an immac-
ulate personality. The rainbow, as an allusion to the overall
developmental process, already exists, but it is far above her.
However, she holds a black fish in her left hand, which Jung
interprets as the Makara (Leviathan) of the Svadhisthana
chakra.[14] So, in this picture, this woman is unconsciously expressing that she has opened herself to the individuation
process and is standing on the threshold of the next chakra.

Figure 11.   A picture drawn by a patient in the root-chakra phase.

The exercises that follow here and each of the remaining sections in this part of the book are meant to serve the following purpose. First, when you practice these exercises, you are meditating on a particular chakra and are reminded of the psychological meaning of these chakras. For example, when you do the Polarity chakra exercise, you can be reminded of the polarities, or the shadow aspects, of the psyche. In addition, when you say the words and do the exercise, you are involving both body and mind. If you meditate on "As in Heaven, so on Earth," you can *feel* the third eye, which is connected to this sentence. Your body becomes involved with the chakra, allowing it to develop. This will also become apparent when you work with the Lord's Prayer later on in the book.

Exercise to Develop the Root Chakra

- With your arms extended (palms facing downward), do a knee bend. (See figure 12.)

- Imagine that you are blessing the earth.

- With each individual knee bend, think or say:

  I am earth.
  I am rooted in the earth.
  The earth supports me.
  The earth is my mother.
  I return to the earth.

- When you rise and stand up, be conscious of this thought:

  I live in this
  *   world.*
  I live in the here
  *   and now.*
  I tackle the task
  *   that is now*
  *   laid before*
  *   me.*
  I take care of
  *   what needs to*
  *   be taken care*
  *   of now.*

Figure 12. Knee bends that reach out to Earth.

- Repeat this exercise as often as it feels right.

The Polarity Chakra—
Svadhisthana (2nd Chakra)

Figure 13.   The symbol of the polarity chakra.

Svadhisthana means "one's own living space" (*Sva* = what belongs to me, *sthan* = living space). This chakra symbolizes something that also still belongs to us—namely, the area of the unconscious. Our overall personality includes not only the world of consciousness but also the world of the unconscious. Whatever emerges from my unconscious mind are characteristics that also belong to me. My "own living space" is therefore the area of consciousness and the unconscious—the entire sphere. (See figure 6, page 33.) This no longer just involves the illuminated disk on the sphere: the second chakra also involves the area of the unconscious. The world of consciousness (the root chakra) is added to the world of the unconscious. This is why it is called the "polarity" chakra because it now includes the counterpole.

The illustration (figure 13, page 41) shows six petals upon which the next six letters of the Sanskrit alphabet are written. So there are now two more petals than in the root chakra, which only has four. However, there is a four-petal difference between the Svadhisthana diagram and the next chakra (Manipura). As I said earlier, the chakras that are differentiated from each other only by two petals are more closely related than the chakras that have a difference of four petals. The root chakra and the polarity chakra belong together in the respect that whatever is contained in the root chakra becomes apparent in the polarity chakra— namely, the concealed and unconscious elements.

In figure 13 (page 41) the unconscious is symbolized by the crescent moon. The moon is a polarity of the sun. Even in the story of Creation in the Bible, it says: "The greater light [sun] rules the day, the lesser light [moon] rules the night" (Genesis 1:16).[1] The night and the moon are symbols of the unconscious. When Jung says that the second center bears all the characteristics of the unconscious, he means that the unconscious behaves in a way that is complementary to the conscious attitude.[2] This means that whatever is large in the conscious mind is small in the unconscious; whatever is masculine in the conscious mind is feminine in the unconscious; whatever is noble in the conscious mind is not so noble in the unconscious.

We also encounter the opposites in fairy tales. The dwarfs, who are small and frequently despised, are usually the smart ones in the fairy tales, while the giants, who are large and impressive, are usually the fools. The situation is also similar in dreams. What we reject in our conscious minds encounters us in dreams as something that belongs to us. This also applies to the sea-monster Makara in figure 13, the illustration of the polarity chakra. The Makara, or Leviathan, as it is called in the Bible, is the name for the devouring monster of the depths. Jung writes: "When we leave Muladhara and reach Svadhisthana, the powers that have supported us up to now take on a different face. When we enter the unconscious, whatever supported and held us in the conscious world becomes our worst enemy. The Leviathan in the depths is the same as the elephant on Earth. But what was a blessing on Earth becomes a curse in the unconscious. The Makara is once again the elephant, but with negative aspects. So the kind mother who has lovingly raised her child can also become the devouring mother from whom the child must separate at the beginning of adult life."[3] We encounter the devouring mother in the fairy tale of Hansel and Gretel in the form of a witch, who is first the nourishing and giving woman, but then becomes the devourer. Jung wrote that whoever attempts to leave the world in order to penetrate the unconscious will have the elephant (in the form of Makara) working against him- or herself.[4] When we go into the unconscious, it isn't difficult at first to pass by the monster, but things look different when we want to return—we walk into the open jaws of the Leviathan. The sea monster is therefore dangerous for those who have become involved with the unconscious and then want to return. They discover that this is almost impossible.

In this context, Jung remembers the medieval tale of "The Dream of Poliphilo." A monk travels through a dark and unfamiliar forest (Jung interprets this as a journey into the unconscious) and gets lost. Then he meets a wolf. The monk is terrified at first, but then follows the wolf as it leads him to a spring. (Jung sees this as a symbol of baptism.) The monk drinks from the spring and continues on his way. Yet, he suddenly has an uneasy feeling and becomes afraid. He wants to turn around and go back. As he turns to take the path back, a dragon blocks the way so that he cannot return.

Jung interprets this dragon as the kundalini forcing us to continue on the path of the great adventure. We may then ask, "Why did I get myself involved in such an adventure?" But if we actually were to give up, our life would then become meaningless. It would lose its fragrance. On the other hand, continuing on the path into the unknown and into the adventure of life makes life worth living. The kundalini is the divine impulse that drives us onward.[5]

The Svadhisthana is associated with the water element and the letter at the center is *Va (Vam)*, representing the water deity, Varuna. Hauer believes that the eight outer and inner lotus petals produce "the feeling of moving water."[6] We can practically see how the water moves in waves toward the inside and the outside.

Water dreams occur quite frequently. These are usually dreams that belong to the polarity chakra. If, on the other hand, we dream of solid objects, these are usually Muladhara dreams. Through our dreams, we can also recognize the chakra themes with which our soul is occupied. (Experience has shown that the lower chakras appear more often in dreams than the higher.) Jung says that the Christian baptism is a passage into water. He refers to the baptistry of the Orthodox Church in Ravenna where, among the four frescos, there is also a fresco of the sinking Peter—an indication of the devouring aspect of water.[7]

Jung thinks that today we say "analysis" instead of Makara (or Leviathan) since analysis means rebirth and the danger of drowning in the unconscious.[8] Analysis is not a pleasant stroll, but an involvement with life and death.[9]

The ancient sun myth is a symbolic depiction of baptism and the polarity chakra. The old sun drowns in the

Western sea, then takes its nighttime sea journey, and is re-born in the morning in the East. So the experience of being devoured is part of the polarity chakra, but it also includes the knowledge of rebirth.[10]

PROJECTION

The polarity—whatever has remained unconscious in the root chakra, namely the shadow—shows up in the polarity chakra. The shadow is always unconscious, or it would not be the shadow!

Above all, the shadow manifests itself in our projec-tions.[11] Projection has a very important function because we get to know ourselves through it. Consequently, it is impor-tant that we don't immediately block projections and say, "I shouldn't have such ugly thoughts about other people!" We should, and even must, have them! If we do not do this, then we prevent ourselves from truly getting to know our-selves. Sometimes I have the impression that our fellow human beings are only here so we can become annoyed with them (or admire them!), which allows us to get to know ourselves better.

We perceive our own shadow in an especially vivid way during projection. This is why listening to people complain about others is so informative. When they do this, they show themselves as clearly as an X ray. They reveal who they really are. When politicians become insulting toward each other, the shadow becomes quite easy to recognize. Whatever gets us emotionally excited about others (and it is important for the emotions to be involved!) is our own shadow. Through projection, whatever also exists within us becomes visible. Whatever we keep under our hat becomes visible in projection. Then we show the characteristics that do not fit into our persona. Projecting—as necessary as it may be—is also dangerous. When we do not withdraw our projections, we saddle someone else with something that belongs to us in the long run. Since it annoys us so much, we project it onto others. All of the pogroms that have taken place in the course of history were the consequences of projections. Projections that we do not acknowledge also have the effect of allowing our shadow aspects to thrive unhindered in our psyche. They can develop there and run wild, which is extremely harmful for our psychic (of the psyche) development, and prevents us from becoming whole.

One particularly dangerous consequence of projection is the alienation of other people through projectiles that we shoot into them when projecting. The peril of such a projectile was already recognized in the Old Testament. In Psalms, it says: "Their tongue is as an arrow shot out; it speaketh deceit; one speaketh peaceably to his neighbor with his mouth, but in heart he layeth his wait" (Jeremiah 9:8).

Jean-Paul Sartre impressively describes the damage done by such murderous projectiles in the life of a human being by using Gustave Flaubert as an example.

The child Gustave Flaubert had difficulties learning the alphabet. His mother had taught his older brother reading and writing in no time. But she failed with Gustave. After a while, she believed she had to reveal this shortcoming to his father. The father, with the martial name of Achille-Cleophas Flaubert, who was the senior physician at the hospital of Rouen, received the mother's news in a very ungracious manner. He looked at his second son with the unerring eye of a surgeon. The boy sat dreaming, sucking his thumb, in a corner. The fatherly judgment was merciless. He turned to the mother and said, "We have an idiot in the family." The boy internalized what his father said—it became his law in life. Gustave became a great failure in the eyes of his family. He was not capable of leading an independent life. As long as his mother lived, she treated him like someone in need of nursing. After his father's judgmental glance, the future of an active professional life was blocked for the son. He fled into neurosis and the world of the imagination.[12]

This was his salvation. Max Frisch described a similar alienation through projectiles in Andorra.

The opposites that we encounter in the polarity chakra can naturally also have a positive character. When we do not recognize these "positive" personality aspects as belonging to us, then we may also project them onto our fellow human beings.

In the positive projection, we project an aspect of the personality that we view as positive, according to our value system, onto another human being. While the negative projection leads to the demonizing of the other person, the positive projection leads to idolizing or idealizing the other. Positive projections embody their own possibilities, which we have not yet recognized. Just as we project the negative shadow on someone else because we do not recognize it within ourselves, there are also positive aspects that we do not recognize within ourselves, but only perceive through their reflection in others.

However, positive projections can be just as dangerous as the negative ones. What we feel to be "positive" or "negative" is always related to our own value system. Something that is positive for one can be negative for the other person, and vice versa.[13] If an individual is idolized by many others, projections are also shot into this person. These alienate and make the person into something that he or she is not. This is especially dangerous for children. In earlier times it was probably more customary for adults to project "positive" qualities onto their children, seeing them as especially talented people who should become something that the parents were not capable of achieving themselves.

I remember a man—he was in his mid-40s at the time—whose father had wanted to become a mechanical engineer, but who didn't achieve this goal for some reason or another. As a result, the man wanted his son to take up this profession. Through his projection, the father had practically forced the son to follow this career path, even though the son tended more toward artistic abilities and would have liked to learn an artistic profession. The son ultimately became a mechanical engineer. He worked in a factory for a good salary, but he was not happy. The desire to do artistic work continued to live on within him. Shortly after his father died, he gave up his position and entered into an artistic field. Now he is happy in his new profession—even though he earns less than before.

The contents of the unconscious and shadow aspects are not only revealed in projections, but also in dreams. For example, Dorothea, a 45-year-old woman, was a capable worker for a Christian congregation. She was generally valued, popular, and well-adjusted. One day, she decided to go to therapy to deal with some personal problems. After beginning analysis, she had the following dream: she saw herself lying down—without hands, without feet, without a face—motionless in front of the altar in a church where a rigid wooden cross stood.[14]

In discussing the dream, it became clear that Dorothea had a very authoritarian and petty father. There were many commandments and prohibitions, and the father zealously monitored their observance. The smallest act of disobedience was severely punished. For Dorothea, God was her father magnified into infinity. God was—like the father—a strict observer who did not overlook any small "sins." Some months after this dream, Dorothea remembered that, when she was a child, her mother had read her a particular fairy tale over and over—Ludwig Bechstein's fairy tale, "God Everywhere." In this fairy tale, Goergel, a little boy, feels hungry and wants to eat something while his parents are gone. He wants some of the cream that his mother keeps in the cellar. Bechstein writes, "Goergel began to eat the cream. But when he was in the middle of licking and slurping, a mighty peal of thunder rolled over him and lightning flashed through the cellar wall, so that the room became very bright and fiery. A man came out of the corner of the cellar, walked toward Goergel, and sat down right across from him. He had two fiery eyes, which he continuously blazed at the cream pot so Goergel could no longer move a finger because of his fright; he stayed there, sitting very still." This situation was illustrated in Dorothea's fairy-tale book (see figure 14, page 50).

The parents return, look for Goergel, and finally find him in the cellar. They opened the cellar door and looked, as Goergel still sat there rigidly with the cream pot in his hand. As soon as he heard the sound and saw his mother, he was startled, his body jerked, and he cried. The mother took the half-empty cream pot out of his hand, lead him out of the cellar, and gave him a well-deserved spanking. But Goergel never nibbled on sweets again his entire life. And later, if someone wanted to talk him into doing something wrong,

Figure 14.   Goergel meeting God.

he always said, "I won't do it, I won't go with you. God Everywhere sees it. God be with me!" And he became a very upright and well-behaved man.

In her dream, Dorothea apparently encounters the "God" of this fairy tale, who is intensified even more through her father's behavior. Like Goergel, Dorothea lays rigid in front of the altar, the cross above her—rigid like the frog god. The dream shows what this image of God has done to her soul. While Dorothea has externally become an "upright and well-behaved" woman, because of her fear of the God who sees everything, and is a valued worker in a Christian church, she feels increasingly paralyzed within, unable to take her own steps. She has no feet, she is incapable of acting independently; she has no hands, she is incapable of showing her true face; she has no face. This paralysis ultimately led to such pronounced physical and psychological symptoms that she sought a cure.

Dorothea's dream is a typical polarity chakra dream. While she told the children entrusted to her as a Sunday

School teacher about the "loving" God who forgives us our sins, in the dream, the opposite emerges from her unconscious—as the unmerciful "God" who ruthlessly punishes even the smallest lapses.

Exercise to Develop the Polarity Chakra

- Stretch your right hand in an upward direction—as high as possible. At the same time, stretch your left hand downward—as low as possible. Think or speak these words while you do this: "I am stretched between above and below."

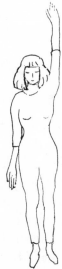

- Then stretch your left hand upward and the right hand downward, and think or speak these words, "I am stretched between right and left."

- Change the position again —as often as it feels right to you—and continue to think of the polarities between which you are stretched, such as, "I am stretched between light and dark, between day and night, between eternity and time, between matter and spirit, between frustration and joy in life, etc."

Figure 15. Acting out the opposite.

The Solar Plexus Chakra—Manipura(3rd Chakra)

Figure 16.   The symbol of the solar plexus chakra.

Now we come to the solar plexus chakra—*Manipura*. *Manipura* means "City of Jewels" (*Mani* = jewel, *pura* = city). Manipura is the fire center of the body. According to the Indian perspective, this is the fire of the god Shiva, who destroys everything in order to create it anew. As I mentioned earlier, Jung thinks that, "in Manipura, passion and sexuality, the will to power, and all the emotional demons break loose. After the baptism, we go directly to Hell. Hell is the City of Jewels—A horrible paradox. But what is a person who does not stand in the fire? Where there is no fire, there is also no light."[1]

The solar plexus chakra has ten petals. There are ten more letters of the Sanskrit alphabet written on them. Manipura has four petals more than the polarity chakra and just two less than the heart chakra. As I mentioned earlier, the chakras that are differentiated by just two petals are closer together. Just like the polarity chakra is the development and complement of the root chakra, the solar plexus chakra finds its fulfillment in the heart chakra.

The illustration of the solar plexus chakra (figure 16, page 52) has the letters *RA (RAM),* which stand for fire, at its center. Manipura is the fire center and the third chakra; the 3 is the number of movement. This is emphasized by the triangle in the middle. The movement is also expressed by the three T-shaped structures on the sides of the triangle. They symbolize a sun wheel that can move from right to left and from left to right. Here is the dream of a well-groomed 50-year-old man.

> On the street, I encounter a grimy figure in dirty clothes and a gloomy look. I react with disdain and flee into my house. I barely have the door closed behind me, and then the house begins to turn—to the left—to the right—to the left—to the right—continuously alternating. When it finally comes to a standstill, I carefully look out the widow. I see that the grimy man is standing in front of the door to my house. He now has my facial features and doesn't look all that gloomy anymore.

Jung gives the Manipura symbol an original meaning. He says that the three Ts appeared to him like the handles on a triangular cooking pot (which he associates with the cooking pot of alchemy). "The Manipura fire is a type of kitchen, just like the stomach is the kitchen of the body where the food is heated with blood and the meals are prepared. We could say that cooking precludes a part of digestion."[2]

The Manipura chakra is the last chakra beneath the diaphragm. In India, the diaphragm is compared to the surface of Earth. The chakras below it are considered the "lower" chakras.

The animal of the Manipura chakra symbol is the ram, which is associated with this chakra. The ram is linked with fire. In India, it belongs to Agni, the God of Fire. In astrology, the ram (Aries) is also a fire sign. The ram and fire indicate a sacrificial cult, which we also encounter in the Old Testament. Sacrifice means killing in order to live. A sacrificial animal (the ram was quite frequently a sacrificial animal) is killed so that those making the sacrifice can live. The idea of a proxy is contained in this act in the knowledge that death is a precondition for life. This is why this chakra includes dying and resurrection. According to the Indian interpretation, meditating on this chakra means destroying the power and creating it anew.[3] The sun wheel's turning from right-to-left means "going into death." The left-to-right turning of the sun wheel means "going into life."

PRODUCING ENERGY

Energy is produced in the fire center of Manipura. While we absorb energy from the outside through the other chakras, the solar plexus chakra also directly creates energy. This was especially emphasized in Tibet, where particular attention was paid to the energy that is created in the solar plexus chakra. A Tibetan text reports the following exercise.

The students sit naked in the lotus position. Linen cloths are dipped in icy water. Each of the men wraps up in a wet towel and must dry it on his own body. As soon as it is dry, it is once again dipped in the water and dried again. This process is repeated for an entire night until the break of day. The person who has dried the most linen cloths on his body is honored as the winner of the competition.

It has been reported that a Tibetan named Arepa once spent an entire winter in a cave warming himself with just the heat from his own solar plexus, and this made it possible for him to survive. We may also experience the solar plexus chakra "heat up" during autogenic training. If we imagine that the forehead is cool and the solar plexus is warm, we can experience that a distinctly tangible heat is created in Manipura through the imagination. By means of visualization, it is also possible to direct currents of energy from the solar plexus to the sick areas of our body. This supports the healing process.

The solar plexus chakra is the seat of the emotions. Things often get "hot" here. For example, we say, "I'm burning with anger." Love can also be hot and burn like fire. When we repress our feelings, they upset our stomach, which in turn leads to various health disorders. Jung writes,

the fire, here, then has the meaning of the *Manipura* center, and that has a healing effect because the things that were separate and contradictory are fused together, it is a melting together; there is also the idea of the alchemical pot in which substances are mixed and melted together.[4]

The unconscious mind has no opportunity to reach into consciousness if this consciousness does not open up to allow energy to pass through. The fire of Manipura has a healing effect because things that have been separated and that were opposing each other are now fused together. This is the actual meaning of the solar plexus chakra in view of the individuation process: what was separated before, the shadow that was projected, is brought together with the ego. A *coniunctio oppositorum* occurs, a unification of opposites.

An example of this is demonstrated in a report by a 47-year-old woman.

> After I recently felt the old familiar pain in my soul, yesterday I felt a sharp pain in my stomach, as if a fire were burning. I was on the way to a team meeting, and was very touchy toward the women on the team. I thought that Hanna and Beate had joined forces against me. Erna is reserved and unclear, which I feel is directed toward me. I think that she has something against me. Ms. Conrad justifies herself, which I feel to be an attack against me. I also think that Lore will not support me. I have the fantasy that they all think I certainly will not come to the club evening. They are all against me, even Berta and Susanne have things to say against me. The fire in me is now so strong that I can practically visualize it in front of me. I see a golden-yellow copper kettle hanging above the fire. All the figures that I feel are attacking me in the outside world are in this kettle. They are in the kettle above the fire. I recognize that these are my inner figures that are boiling. Ms. Conrad, who justifies herself; Erna, who is so distant and always insulted; Beate, who claims things she doesn't know anything about; Hanna,

who girlishly joins forces with her; Berta and Su-
sanne, who complain so much. Yes, these are figures within me that I know very well.[5]

WITHDRAWING PROJECTIONS—
INTEGRATING THE OPPOSITES

The focus of the solar plexus chakra is the integration of
the unification of opposites that has emerged in the polarity chakra. "I recognize that my shadow belongs to me."
This is not yet the case in the polarity chakra. In the polarity chakra, we reject the shadow and project it onto others.
But by projecting it, we endow the counterpole with emotions. We react emotionally to others, and this is very important. This is why projection is significant, and cannot be
skipped over or covered up. As a result, we heat up something within us so that it can be cooked afterward. Since
projections produce emotions, they are no longer "events"
that take place only in the mind. ("But that's just a projection!") Instead, we get annoyed to pieces about the people
we project upon. That's very important. Only that which is
experienced emotionally in the polarity chakra can be
cooked and processed in the solar plexus.

The solar plexus chakra is involved in withdrawing
projections, which means integrating the opposites. The
polarity is generally not "bad," but just one-sided. By bringing it home, we free it from its one-sidedness. Then it frequently turns into pure gold. It becomes something that can
enrich and enhance our life. This is a matter of looking at
characteristics that we judge to be negative and perceiving
that they belong to us, then integrating them. This allows a
piece of the wholeness to be realized within our souls.

What we had previously separated from ourselves is now a part of us. In addition, we become a bit more compassionate toward the people upon whom we have previously projected. When we discover a characteristic within ouselves that we previously judged as negative in others, we can no longer judge the others to the same degree that we did previously, when we thought that the rejected characteristics only existed within the others, and not within ourselves.

This also applies to positive projections. When we admire other people and discover "positive" attributes in them that we think we don't have within ourselves, then this has an important function: something within ourselves is activated that was previously dormant. Withdrawing a positive projection means that our sense of self-worth is strengthened and we protect ourselves against overestimating others.

When a projection is withdrawn, this means that wholeness (polarity) is created from two cases of one-sidedness (polarization). Here are some examples to clarify this situation. For example, when a person is a daredevil, it is quite possible that he despises cowardly people who do not have the confidence to do certain things that he does, so he projects his cowardice upon others. He may bungee-jump off of a bridge. Another person may be afraid to do this, so the daredevil feels contempt toward him and thinks this individual is a coward. However, the daredevil is basically despising his own cowardice, and projecting it onto the other. When someone is especially daring, this recklessness is usually a defense against his own cowardice, which is also inside of him. If he withdraws the projection and recognizes his own inner cowardice, then the two extremes of "recklessness" and "cowardice" become a virtue—namely, bravery. A "courageous person" can also behave like a daredevil when he, for example, rescues another person. Then he is doing something he would normally not do. A "courageous person" can also be "cowardly" (in the opinion of the daredevil) when he avoids unnecessarily endangering himself. Courage keeps the two poles together.

The situation is similar with stinginess. The miserly person generally despises the spendthrift (and the spendthrift despises the miserly person!). And why is a person stingy? Because he or she is afraid of personal wastefulness, which lies deep within the soul. And vice versa: the spendthrift fights the stinginess that is also within. When we bring together the wastefulness and the stinginess, the result is the proper approach to money. Then, when necessary, we can spend money and be generous; but we can also save and handle money wisely.

Bringing together the polarities applies to many things, including the theme of "closeness and distance." Some people express too much closeness—they don't have a "front yard" and want to embrace everyone, while others maintain too much distance. When we bring the opposites together, the proper relationship between closeness and distance arises.[6]

Moreover, bringing together the opposites means taking the concerns of the surrounding world seriously (these are taken seriously in a one-sided way in the persona), as well as the concerns of our own psyche. Individuation is the midway point between collectivism and individualism. Both the needs and rights of the collective and the needs and rights of the individual are taken seriously. On the other hand, one-sided situations expressed in collectivism and individualism can be avoided.

The meaning of integrating the shadow becomes clear in figure 17 (page 60), the picture drawn by a patient, and published in C. G. Jung's CW 13. The woman no longer stands, bright in the light "above" the darkness as in her first picture.[7] Something has changed within her during the course of the self-actualization.[8]

Jung describes the change. The woman is now in a sitting position, which means a shift downward. She was pre-

Figure 17.   Self-actualization.

viously just oriented in an upward direction. The black earth that was beneath her feet in the previous picture can now be found within her body in the form of a black ball. And it is near the Manipura, which coincides with the solar plexus. This means that the dark principle, or shadow, has now been integrated and is felt to be a type of center within the body.[9] The many birds circling the tree means that we have already reached the transition to the heart chakra, which is associated with air and, therefore, the birds.[10] The branches, which were previously thin twigs growing out of the woman, have now developed much more strongly. The rainbow, as a symbol of becoming whole, is no longer high above the woman, but inside of her. This woman has apparently withdrawn her projections and discovered the darkness within herself.

However, there are two limitations related to withdrawing projections. First, there is a quantitative limitation: we cannot integrate everything. There are negative things that we may alarmingly recognize in others as if in a mirror (for example, on television and in the newspaper) such as a murderer shadow, or an extremely sadistic shadow. There are aspects of the personality that we can recognize as being part of ourselves, but we are not permitted to live them. There are things that should not be lived out.

But what do we do when we are so angry with another person that we would really like to kill this person? One possibility is expressing this anger in a letter. However, it is important not to send the letter; we can write everything in the letter, but not mail it. We can also write letters to people who have died (such as parents). Once we have written everything down, it is good to burn it (perhaps in a ritual). Fire has transformational power. In this way, we can take a murderous or sadistic shadow seriously without having to live it out.

There is a second limitation: a strong ego is required for integration. People with weak egos will—rightfully—protect themselves against too much knowledge of the shadow, or too much shadow integration, since they already feel bad and worthless. When they are then burdened with something else that they cannot bear, this can do damage to the psyche. Jung compares our conscious mind with a boat that floats on the sea of the unconscious. People sit in this boat and fish. Jung says that these people should not bring more fish (meaning the unconscious contents) out of the depths and into the boat than the boat can carry, since it would otherwise sink.[11] This is a very important aspect. It is not a matter of bringing no fish into the boat, but no more fish than the boat can carry. When people are forced to integrate more "negative" personality aspects than they can accept, it is possible that they will "sink" and became seriously ill.

When integrating a positive projection, weak egos are subject to the danger of inflation, which is also dangerous. People may then identify with an idol, and think that they are a goddesses or gods.

People who tend to lose touch with reality need the appropriate ballast to keep them grounded. For example, the apostle Paul says, "And lest I should be exalted above measure through abundance of revelations, there was given to me a thorn in the flesh."[12] The apostle Peter, who had a high task entrusted to him, also had such a thorn, namely, a dark spot in his biography: he had denied Jesus. This followed him for his entire lifetime. Even today, he is still the Peter who denied Jesus. The denial was important for Peter, since this was the only way he could have become the person he became.[13] He needed the ballast. On the other hand, people who have feelings of inferiority must learn to forgive themselves and develop the appropriate sense of self-worth. All of this is part of the Manipura process.

In conclusion, the integration of the contrasexual pole—what Jung has called anima and animus—also belongs to the solar plexus chakra. We encounter the repressed contrasexual pole in dreams in the respective positive or negative figures of the opposite sex. This is how it can be recognized and integrated. When the anima is repressed, it is said that men fall prey to an anima possession. When this happens, men become touchy, depressed, and engage in emotional, thoughtless actions that may take on manic characteristics. In terms of the animus, Jung writes that feminine psychology has a counterpart to a man's anima, which primarily has a quasi-intellectual nature that, when unintegrated, could influence a woman to be obstinate, cold, and completely inaccessible.[14] Although both men and women have an animus, as well as an anima, according to the more recent findings of analytical psychology, we speak of the man's anima and the woman's animus when we talk about the contrasexual pole.

For the anima, Jung differentiates four levels of development for men: the mythological level, such as Eve, an image related purely to biology; the romantic-esthetic aspect, such as Helena as she appears in Goethe's *Faust;* the spiritualized aspect, such as the Virgin Mary; and finally the symbolic level, such as Sophia.[15] M. L. von Franz differentiates the four levels of the animus for a woman in a similar manner: the personification of physical power (the athlete); then she posesses initiative and enterprise (the researcher, inventor, physician); then she becomes "the word" (professors, doctors, and ministers); and the final manifestation is *meaning,* mediating inner, religious experiences and she may be idolizing gurus or guides of the soul.[16]

Manipura is the chakra that plays a special role in every self-actualization process. Manipura characterizes a lengthy process that involves a constant "up and down" and "back and forth" until the lowest point has finally been passed and something new emerges.

Exercise to Develop the Solar Plexus Chakra

- Swing both arms to the left and to the right, left and right, as you think or speak: "I connect the right side with the left side, the upper with the lower, the spirit with matter, Heaven with Earth, my feminine side with my masculine side, and so forth."

- Do this exercise as long as it feels right.

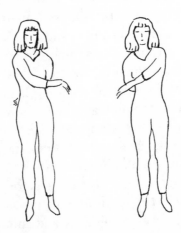

Figure 18.   Connecting the opposites.

The Heart Chakra—
Anahata (4th Chakra)

Figure 19.   The symbol of the heart chakra.

The Sanskrit name of the heart chakra is Anahata. *Anahata* means "unbeaten." Once again, we can recognize the relationship between the European languages and Sanskrit. For example, an analphabet (illiterate) is a non-alphabet. In the same way, An-ahata is something that is not beaten. According to the Indian perspective, this chakra has a vibration that does not occur through an external effect ("beating"); instead, it is a primal vibration. This vibration comes from God, according to the Indian viewpoint, who is "the not-born and the not-dying, eternal vibration."[1] This "divine" vibration is the energy that manifests itself as elemental particles, from which matter is created. We can compare the unbeaten vibration with the original light that is described at the beginning of the Bible, "And God said,

Let there be light; and there was light" (Genesis 1:3). This original light is not at all related to the light of the heavenly bodies, which were only created on the fourth day. Instead, it is a light that we also see in our dreams. When everything is dark, when we have closed our eyes, we still see everything as bright as day in our dreams. This is an inner light, a primal light.

Jung says that the first flash of the Self occurs in the heart chakra. So we come out of the purely material, superficial world and enter into the cryptic world. Something new happens. It is interesting to note that there is another, small chakra (beneath the heart chakra in figure 19) between the solar plexus chakra and the heart chakra. It is not one of the seven main chakras, but practically a bonus.

This is the "wishing tree." The following concept is behind it: when we have experienced the first three chakras, when we have taken the area of everyday reality seriously in the root chakra over and over again, when we have encountered the shadow and projection in the polarity chakra, and when we have withdrawn projections and connected the polarities in Manipura (implying a dynamic polarity has been created from the one-sided polarization), then we have come far enough so that our heart's desires of are fulfilled, meaning that our wishes are no longer infected by shadow aspects.

A Sanskrit commentary says, "The divine wishing tree gives more than any wish could imagine." There is a deep wisdom revealed here—that wishes from the heart are different from what we wish for with our conscious mind. Only when we have gone through Manipura do our heart's desires come to light at all. Before this point, they were buried under ego wishes and projections. So we did not even know what we actually wanted until now. The wishes of the mind are not fulfilled because they do not fulfill us, because they are not our actual wishes. The heart's desires arise when the opposing poliarity is no longer there. The non-integrated polarity suppresses what we actually want. Even in the Psalms, we can read: "Delight thyself also in the Lord, and he shall give thee the desires of thine heart," (Psalms 37:4).

Twelve petals can be seen in the Anahata chakra symbol—two more than in Manipura. Manipura and Anahata belong together since the peace of the heart chakra is the goal of the movement in the solar plexus chakra. The twelve petals of the Anahata symbol are a symbol of the "peace" that is not a static but a dynamic calm. The twelve is 4×30, which means that repose (4) and movement (3) come together. So the heart chakra is both movement and repose. This is also expressed by the six-rayed star, the symbol of the heart chakra. This star is frequently called the Star of David. However, it has no connection with David whatsoever. In Judaism, it appears for the first time in the fourteenth century on a Jewish gravestone in Bohemia. But the symbol itself does not come from Judaism. This star is a much older chakra symbol. It also appears as a Alemannian heraldic symbol. Consequently, the Star of David is a very profound human symbol.

This six-rayed star is composed of a feminine and a masculine triangle. The masculine triangle points upward. (Incidentally, this is the only masculine triangle that appears in chakra symbolism.) The feminine triangle points downward. The bottom and the top come together here. It is a dynamic movement from "below" to "above" and from above to below. The movement from below to above is reminiscent of the hole that is bored from the conscious level to the unconscious so that a unification of conscious and unconscious can occur. The star is both repose and movement at the same time. Movement is expressed through the two triangles, but the star expresses repose in its entirety. In *The Gospel According to Thomas,* God is described as movement and rest.[2] The six-rayed star is therefore a symbol of peace, the nature of which is dynamic repose.[3]

The letter in the middle of the Anahata diagram is called *yam* and means "air." Jung says: "A flashing of the self, which is something completely different than what we are, occurs in the heart chakra. The ego is just a little appendage of the self. The ego always remains in the root chakra." As the center of consciousness, the ego remains stuck there. Yet, when rising to the fourth chakra, it suddenly discovers the self. "When the self directs us, then we are like strangers,"[4] which means we feel something different here, something unfamiliar to us, that connects the conscious mind and the unconscious with each other.

The animal in the heart chakra is the antelope. The antelope is the symbol of air that is connected with Earth. When a herd of antelope flees, it practically flies. An antelope can jump distances of up to twenty feet long and six feet high. It is virtually an air animal, but must always come back down to Earth. The animal therefore bears the symbolism of connecting below and above within—which is repeated in the horns that point upward and the hooves that point downward. No matter how "high" we climb up the chakra ladder, it is important not to lose contact with the ground beneath our feet.

What does this concept mean in psychological terms? Jung said that we move backward and forward. When we move to Manipura, there is no more identification with emotions, but emotions are virtually observed from above. In Anahata, we *have* emotions; in Manipura we *are* emotions."[5] According to C. G. Jung's opinion, native peoples live in the Manipura state, which is why they need rituals. Rituals prevent emotions from degenerating into murder and killing. In some parts of the world, where these rituals no longer exist, there are permanent wars today because there has been no further development toward Anahata. By accepting the emotions of Manipura as belonging to us, and connecting them with a dynamic polarity, we succeed in rising above them. The storm in the valley of Manipura may still be there, but we stand above it in Anahata.

One example for the transition from the solar plexus chakra to the heart chakra has been published in my book on the Lord's Prayer.[6] Here I discuss the dream of a man who, at the end of a long Manipura phase, dreams that he swims in the sea not far from the coast. Suddenly, he sees a large, black animal in front of him, reaching for him with its long tentacles. He attempts to escape from this animal by swimming backward, and simultaneously makes wavelike motions with the back of his hand to drive the animal away. A little later, he looks up and sees to his amazement that the threatening animal has changed into a mandala. Slowly and quietly, almost solemnly, it swims toward him.

A joyful amazement, combined with a numinous feeling, flows through him. The figure of the mandala is so clear that he could still see it quite precisely in front of him and he draws it. On the basis of this dream, this man realized that the adversity and threats of his life ultimately serve the process of becoming whole.

Figure 20. The tentacles become a mandala.

Figure 21.   The man-
dala of achievement.

The "wholeness" experienced in the heart chakra is the result of a process that takes place in Manipura. This is naturally always just a partial process of becoming whole, a resting-place on the path. In his *Vision Seminars,* Jung focused on the transition between one chakra and the other, especially on the relationship between Manipura and Anahata. He said, for example, that on each level of consciousness, the old mystery of the light and attacks of the darkness are repeated. Each new level means the increasing of light, but every little increase of light can be attacked by the relative darkness of the previous state. This means that when we leave the area of Manipura—which is a lower level—and rise up to the higher level above the diaphragm, to Anahata, then despite the fact that Manipura is a shining sun, it is still darkness in comparison to the strange new light of Anahata.[7]

While, on the one hand, Jung emphasizes the danger that we may be devoured and injured through the descent into a level of consciousness that we have already experienced, he emphasizes on the other hand that there is also a conscious return to an earlier state, which I call "progressive regression"[8] and is also called a "regression in the service of the ego" by neo-Freudians.[9] Such a conscious return can mean a *reculer pour mieux sauter,* "going backward in order to get a running start for a leap forward." Similar forms of regression also appear in our dreams. Jung views this conscious regression in the following manner: "You can descend into the abysmal water to be healed, the baptismal water being the *uterus resurrectionis* (the uterus of resurrection) where you are made whole again; or you can go into the fire. John the Baptist said of Christ: 'He will baptize you with the Holy Ghost and with fire.' The two forms of baptism refer to the two lower centers; in the fire you can be made whole, and water is still better because it is deeper down. You could not get much further without getting into the earth and then you would be practically dead. Death has been understood to be the complete cure. . . . But the figurative death in the water and the death or wounding in the fire also mean regeneration, because in going back to any state when the ego consciousness is not, there is regeneration."[10]

I once had a conversation with a Native American shaman. He said to me, "When I have to make a difficult decision, I go into the sweat lodge at sunset. I stay there the night and leave again at sunrise." The sweat lodge is a small, igloo-shaped circular building that depicts the womb. It is very dark and narrow in a sweat lodge. At the center is a circular area in which red-hot rocks ("fire") are placed until it is terribly hot in the sweat lodge. These red-hot rocks, which are replaced by a helper from time to time, are repeatedly sprinkled with water ("water") that immediately vaporizes and causes stinging pain on the naked body of the shamans, who sit on the ground ("earth"). The Native American comes into contact with the motherly primal ground. His soul seeks the right answer there, and when he leaves the sweat lodge in the morning (into the cool "air")—which he instinctively does at sunrise—then the sun inside of him also rises. He has found the strength to make the proper decision in the motherly primal ground.[11]

This is the experience of the heart chakra: through the experience of the earth (root chakra), water (polarity chakra), and fire (solar plexus chakra), we attain a new position above everything ("air" = heart chakra). Whatever previously tore us apart inside has now been transformed into the dynamic repose of "peace."

Exercise to Develop the Heart Chakra

- Stretch your arms out to the side.

- Then stretch your arms behind you, without bending the elbows, so that you feel pressure in your shoulder blades.

- Bend your hands backward at the wrists so that you also feel pressure in your hands.

- Now inhale and raise the chest upward and forward (see figure 22). Then bring the palms together in front of the body while exhaling, continuing to keep the arms extended. Slightly round the back in a forward direction (see figure 23).

Figure 22.   Inhale.

Figure 23.   Bring your palms together and exhale.

- While inhaling, bring the arms and hands behind you again and forward again while exhaling.

- While inhaling, think or speak "I open myself to the world."

- While exhaling, think or speak, "I am totally with myself."

- You can also think or speak the following sentences:

  "Peace fills my heart."
  "The polarities within me are united."
  "I stand above the storm in the valley."

  And so forth.

- Repeat this exercise as long as it feels right to you.

The Throat Chakra—
Vishuddhi (5th Chakra)

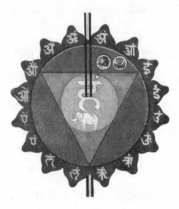

Figure 24.   The symbol of the throat chakra.

The throat chakra is associated with ether, which was known in ancient times as the fifth element, the "quint"-essence. Ether represents the transition to the spiritual world and is no longer directly related to the material world. "It is matter that is not matter."[1] It is the substance of which angels are made.[2] Ether is the firmament that spans the world,[3] and the substance that fills the firma-ment. But it is also the substance of sound. Sounds live in this substance or are formed from it: the music of the spheres and the heavenly chorus remind us of this. The ear is also formed from this substance. "The ear is the *sthula* expression of ether, which is why we can perceive sounds, since these are an expression of the same substance."[4] Through the *tuba auditiva*, the ear is connected with the throat. This means it is also connected with the throat chakra.

All the Sanskrit consonants are written on the petals in the first four chakras. In the throat chakra, the vowels are added. There are sixteen petals with the sixteen Sanskrit vowels, among which is also the "M" since it sounds on its own and is therefore a vowel. The throat chakra is therefore a resonant chakra in which all the vowels sound together. In the chakra symbol, we see a circle in a feminine triangle. This is the only chakra in which the circle is inside the triangle. In the other chakras, the circle is always just on the outside around the triangle. This means that the divine world is now within us. It not only encounters us in the outside world, but we also find it within ourselves. This is a very essential statement for the symbolic meaning of this chakra.

The nature of a symbol is to reveal the divine to us within the earthly realm. This enigmatic reality—Jung calls it the "psychic reality"—is just as real as the superficial, material reality that is encountered in the root chakra. The elephant now appearing for the second time expresses this. The seven trunks show that this development also involves all seven chakras. Jung writes the following about this elephant: The elephant appears again in Vishuddhi. Here we encounter anew the force that has supported us in the world, the insurmountable, sanctifying power of the animal. . . . So the products of our minds are therefore also reality. . . . These are things that the elephant bears in Vishuddhi and turns into reality.[5]

When she was 95 years old, Elisabeth Haich wrote the following sentence in her book on initiation for me: "Imagine the realities, then your ideas will become reality." This is Vishuddhi. "The psychic experiences and not the data of earthly reality are what is real in Vishuddhi. When, for example, we are caused to act in an invincible way or just as compellingly prevented from acting, then we feel the power of the elephant in Vishuddha."[6] The elephant in Vishuddhi reminds us of the daimon of Socrates, who keeps us from taking false paths[7] or the spirit of Jesus, which prevented Paul from taking false paths.[8] For Jung, the world of the Vishuddhi chakra is a world of abstract ideas, "the world where the psyche exists in itself . . . where matter is only a thin skin round an enormous cosmos of psychical realities."[9]

What does this mean? According to Jung, psychic data is not related to the material world. As mentioned in the example above, the annoyance that we feel about someone or something has nothing to do with this person or issue. Instead, it is a phenomenon in itself. I am angry—this is purely subjective.[10] The people we encounter in the outer world are exponents of our own psychic condition (of the psyche).[11] We encounter ourselves in the mirror of the other people and things that we experience. This is the nature of the symbol with which we become involved in the Vishuddhi chakra. When I encounter the light or darkness within the symbol, then I encounter the light or darkness within myself. When I encounter the divine in the symbol, then I encounter the divine within myself.

WHAT IS A SYMBOL?

A symbol depicts something internal in the external world. Through the symbol, we encounter the cryptic within the superficial. Just as we basically only encounter ourselves in other people, we also encounter cryptic reality in the external appearances of this world. In the finite, we encounter the infinite; in the earthly, we encounter the heavenly; in temporality, we encounter eternity. Everything earthly becomes a metaphor. An example of this can be seen in the metaphors of Jesus, which are instructions in symbolic vision: Jesus teaches us to see the heavenly world behind the appearance of the earthly world. Every flower, every sunrise, every encounter with other people become transparent and reveal a larger reality that lies behind it.

The symbol unites two levels. The Greek word *symballein* means "two things that are brought together." When there is only one side, there is no symbol involved. A symbol reveals an eternal meaning in an earthly manifestation. The above and below, the earthly and the heavenly, the material and the spiritual, the temporal and the eternal communicate in symbols. Two levels always encounter each other.

WHAT IS THE DIFFERENCE BETWEEN SYMBOL AND SIGN?

A sign is always clear. It can never be complex, since it will otherwise lose its character as a sign. A sign can also be expressed in words. When we, [in Europe] for example, see a round sign and a diagonal cross on it as a traffic sign, we know that this means "no stopping." We could just as well write "no stopping." If, on the other hand, a cross is in a triangle, then it indicates a crossing. We could also write, "be careful of crossing." Traffic signs, in particular, must be very clear. "No stopping" means "no stopping" and nothing else.

On the other hand, a symbol conveys a complex and enigmatic meaning. It can never be expressed completely in words because it has a surplus of meaning. A symbol is

inexhaustible because it participates in the visible world,
and also in the invisible and unconscious reality. The realm
of the unconscious is inexhaustible.

A symbol means to me whatever it awakens within me.
This is why a symbol cannot be generalized. In the West,
for example, the dragon is usually a negative symbol. However, it is a symbol of good luck in China. Therefore, the
symbol means to me whatever it triggers within me.

A SYMBOL IS LIKE A MIRROR

When I look in a mirror, I see a completely different picture
than another person who looks at himself or herself in the
same mirror. It is the same mirror, but I see myself and the
other person sees himself or herself.

A symbol is an apparent image in which the hidden reality is reflected. This is also the function of the icons in the
worship service of the Orthodox Church. For Orthodox
believers, the icons are not "pictures," but windows through
which Christ, the Virgin Mary, or the saints look. The believers encounter these figures in a very real way through
the icons. When the believers touch the icons, they have a
meaningful contact with the figure that the icons symbolically represent. The Platonic idea/reflection thinking is behind the Orthodox Church's understanding of icons. Plato
says that there is a heavenly archetype for all earthly things
and this archetype is duplicated in the earthly realm.

A symbol has an effect on the observer. When I open
myself for the message of a symbol, something occurs
within me. I encounter the metaphysical reality that lies behind it. The power of the archetype takes effect in the reflection. Let's take the example of a burning candle: it

consumes itself by burning, illuminating, warming, and spreading a cozy or solemn atmosphere. However, behind the fire of the candle is ultimately the fire of the sun, and behind the sun is Christ, who is the archetype of all earthly manifestations and fulfills everything in everything. So just looking at a candle can awaken an entire world of meanings within us.

When we look at earthly things like a symbol, then they become as transparent as a pane of glass, making it possible to look into deeper dimensions.

In the symbol, we experience the visible manifestations as God's messengers. We experience that a messenger of the other world—an angel—comes to meet us. We can never directly perceive the divine. We can only see its reflected splendor, and this occurs through the symbol.

A symbol is never static; it is always dynamic. It is charged with the strength that opens the message of the symbol to the observer, and brings about the meaning of the symbol—which is wholeness. A genuine symbol leads us from its derivatives to the origin. The archetype is truly present in the symbol. Only the symbol can appropriately speak of God because the mystery resonates in the symbol. The symbol contains both the other world and this world. What occurs between light and shadow, what unites the opposites, partakes in both sides. The symbol is the *tertium* in which there is no logic but the living truth and reality. Logic speaks of "either/or," but symbolism means "both/and." Both of these approaches are realities of the soul. Consequently, the scintillating symbol expresses the processes of the soul in a more fitting, complete, and therefore infinitely more distinct way than the clearest term. The symbol awakens premonitions, while the language explains. The symbol strikes many strings of the soul at the same time. Many different things are united into an over-all impression.[12]

The myth and the archetype are part of the symbol as well. The myth also depicts inner reality in the outside world. The myth is a dramatization of the symbol; it is a symbol in the form of a story

Archetypes are also symbols. Jung writes, archetypes "are genuine symbols precisely because they are ambiguous, full of half-glimpsed meanings, and, in the last resort, inexhaustible. The ground principles . . . of the unconscious are indescribable because of their wealth of reference, although in themselves recognizable."[13]

In summary, we could say that a symbol has many meanings. In contrast to a sign, it cannot be expressed in words alone. A symbol awakens thoughts and presentiments. A symbol touches different strings in the human psyche. A symbol is a reflection of the idea behind it. The idea is set into the present in the reflection. In the symbol, we encounter the effective power of the idea. By letting the symbol have its effect upon us, we increasingly become shaped like the idea it represents.

In the path of the chakras, the throat chakra speaks of the intertwining of external and internal reality. It is therefore the "symbol" chakra.

Exercise to Develop the Throat Chakra

- Lift your chin and think or speak these words: "The heavenly . . ."

- Now lower your chin and think or speak these words: ". . . in the earthly . . ."

- Repeat this exercise as long as it feels right for you: "The heavenly in the earthly, the heavenly in the earthly, the heavenly in the earthly," etc.

- Tilt your head to the left and think or speak: "The eternal . . ."

- Then tilt your head to the right and think or speak: ". . . in the temporal."

- Repeat this exercise as long as it feels right for you: "The eternal in the temporal, the eternal in the temporal, the eternal in the temporal," etc.

- You can also do this exercise in a four-beat cycle: chin up—chin down; head to the left—head to the right; and think or speak these words as you do so: "The heavenly in the earthly—the eternal in the temporal."

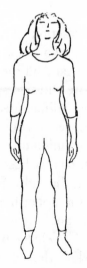 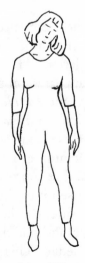

Figure 25.   Lift your chin.   Figure 26.   Tilt your head.

The Third Eye— Ajna (6th Chakra)

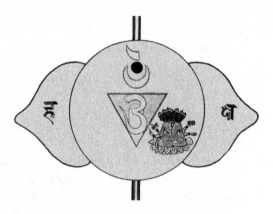

Figure 27.   The symbol of the third eye.

Ajna (pronounced "atschna") means "instruction." The diagram for the third eye chakra has only two lotus petals with two letters. After all the consonants and all the vowels have appeared on the petals, there are still two special letters: *ksa* and *ha*. *Ha* expresses the masculine aspect (on the left side), and *ksa*, the feminine aspect (on the right side). So this chakra symbol involves the union of masculine and feminine. The goddess Shakti has six heads and six hands, three on the left and three on the right. Shakti has now risen into the 6th chakra. In the upper hand on the right side, she holds a book. This book symbolizes knowledge, and this chakra is about the knowledge behind the knowledge. This is not rational knowledge, which comes from masculine energy, but a cryptic feminine knowledge that radiates from Shakti.

The diagram of Shakti is more imposing here than that of Shiva. Shiva is concealed in the central, phallus-shaped symbol *(lingam)* in the feminine triangle that points downward. The syllable in the triangle is an OM opened to the left. *OM* is an all-inclusive word, which is open in this chakra in order to absorb all the chakra experiences and therefore attain its abundance. However, this abundance is only achieved in the crown chakra. The OM in Ajna is an OM opened toward God and perfection.

'What does this chakra mean in psychological terms? We leave the world of the senses in Ajna. There is no longer an outer reality; there is only inner reality. Ajna does not need a symbolic animal, since it differentiates itself from another reality. The psyche does not need to be reflected here, since it now exists alone. Only the psyche is present here.[1] There is also no longer a material counterweight, not even ether. There is, however, a counterpart to this chakra—namely an inner psychic one. There is an objective psychic reality that contrasts to the subjective ego—"that absolute reality where one is nothing but psychic reality."[2] I understand this to mean that this objective reality is the idea of the Self. According to the biblical understanding, this is Christ. He is the idea that comes from "the bosom of the Father." Christ is the "image of God,"[3] but Christ is also simultaneously the archetype of the human being. And we are an image of Christ.[4]

The reality found behind the Self is no longer a subjective, but an objective psychic reality no longer related to the ego. In discussions on this chakra, Jung has said that the reality is God. God is the eternal psychic object, the nonego. It is the reality that will absorb the ego into the nonego.[5]

The opened OM is oriented toward God. It stands for an ego that lets itself be imbued by God. I understand the subjective reality as the subjective "human" spirit that opens up to this objective reality, the "divine" spirit. Paul differentiates between these two types of spirit when he writes: "The Spirit itself [God's spirit] beareth witness with our spirit" (Romans 8:16). It has been said that the human spirit could be called the "God-shaped void," meaning a void in human beings that can only be filled by "God."

As mentioned earlier, Ajna is the chakra of cryptic knowledge, expressed through Shakti, who holds a book in her hand. This is the knowledge behind the knowledge, the view within. The third eye deals with inner vision, inner instruction, and insight. This insight is not imposed upon us by the outside world. It is also not related to any type of law, command, or regulation, but is an inner instruction that occurs.[6] This is the nature of the third eye. Jung expresses this in these terms: "You are not even dreaming of doing anything other than the force [namely, the power of the kundalini in Ajna] is demanding, and the force is not demanding it since you are already doing it, since you are the force."[7]

This is also the human will becoming one with divine will. It is what the Lord's Prayer means when it says: "Thy will be done." It does not mean that I am doing something, but that the will of God occurs without my help. In Ajna, our ego is in harmony with our Self. We act from the core of our being. When this isn't the case, when we are controlled from the outside, then we have not yet reached the state of the Ajna chakra.

Exercise to Develop the Third Eye Chakra

- Turn your eyes upward and feel or imagine the third eye (see figure 28, left). While you do this, think or speak: "As in heaven . . ."

- Then slowly bend downward (see figure 28, right); feel or imagine the third eye while you do this. Think or speak: ". . . so on Earth."

- Slowly continue to bend downward until your finger-tips touch the ground. (If this is difficult to do with extended legs, then you can also slightly bend the knees.)

- Slowly move back up to the original position and re-peat this exercise as long as it feels good to you. In-stead of, "As in heaven—so on Earth," you can also think or say: "As above—so below."

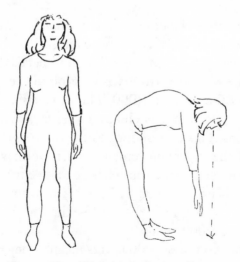

Figure 28.   The third eye exercise.

The Crown Chakra—
Sahasrara (7th Chakra)

Figure 29.   The symbol of the crown chakra.

The symbol of the crown chakra *(Sahasrara)* is the "lotus of a thousand-petals." The entire Sanskrit alphabet is contained twenty times in these thousand petals. Exactly fifty letters are placed in twenty rows around the head, which results in the total of 1,000. The interesting thing about the lotus petals in this chakra is the fact that they point downward. This corresponds to the *enantiodromia,* the reversal of the chakra movement. When we arrive at the top, we return back to the root chakra.[1] The entire abundance that has been achieved indicates a downward direction back to the beginning. OM, as the "highest" syllable, crowns the 1,000 petals.

What do these 1,000 letters mean? They mean everything and nothing. The alphabet is a combination of everything and nothing. What is an alphabet? It is the stringing together of letters, so it is "nothing." And yet, everything is contained within the letters of the alphabet. Since we can combine the letters accordingly, we can express everything there is. This is why the alphabet is well suited for depicting the "everything and nothing" that is summarized within OM.

Regarding this chakra, Jung said that Sahasrara is beyond any type of experience; it is beyond any possible experience. "There is no experience because it is one, it is without a second."[2] The combination of being and not-being in this world is not possible. Existence that is simultaneously also nonexistence is called *Nirvana* in India.

What is Nirvana? As I mentioned earlier, Buddha was once asked whether Nirvana exists. He gave no response. When he was asked whether Nirvana does not exist, he also gave no response. In this way, Buddha wanted to express that every statement about Nirvana is wrong because a statement presupposes a duality. By giving something a name, we distinguish it from something else. Nirvana is everything and nothing. So we can only remain silent.

Sahasrara is the union of all opposites. So it is the "marriage"[3] between masculine and feminine, between Heaven and Earth, between God and human being, between conscious and unconscious, between being and nonexistence. All of this is expressed through the two deities Shiva and Shakti. Everything that exists is contained within Shiva/Shakti—above and below, masculine and feminine, Heaven and Earth, the conscious and unconscious, etc. The union of opposites is the goal of individuation. This goal cannot be ultimately attained here on Earth, but only in respective approaches at certain points.

As you look at the illustration of this chakra, you will see a tiny sign above the OM. Shiva and Shakti are unified within this sign. They have become one perfect unity. In Sanskrit, this sign is called *para bindu*. Within para bindu there is a great void in which there are no longer any differences. We read in a Sanskrit text that this para bindu is as small as one ten-millionth of a tip of hair,[4] which is unimaginably small. This expresses the concept that the largest is contained within the smallest.

In the Jewish Cabala, we encounter a similar concept. The smallest Hebrew letter, the Jod, is the symbol for God in the Cabala. This also means that "the greatest" is contained within the smallest. Jod is the beginning letter of the Hebrew Tetragram of the unspeakable "names" of God.[5] The "name" of God cannot be spoken because it does not participate in the polarity.[6]

We also encounter God—as in the crown chakra—in the Bible as "male and female." So God said, "Let us make man (= "we want to make man") in our image, after our likeness" (Genesis 1:26). In Hebrew, the Elohim, a mono-plural, is behind the "we." In both the Hebrew and Greek text, it says that God created human beings as "masculine and feminine." (Not "as man and woman" as in the King James version of the translation, since that would already be a differentiation. The differentiation in "man" and "woman" results only in the second chapter of Genesis.[7]) The differentiated unity[8] flows into the wholeness of God in the crown chakra.

The thousand lotus petals that point downward symbolize not only the descent (back to the root chakra), but also the cosmic energy that flows downward from the crown chakra. A description of this chakra says, "The cosmic forces flow like a cascade off a person who has arrived in Sahasrara. He is filled by a force that flows off him like a water-fall." This reminds us of what Jesus said about a spirit-filled person, "Out of his heart shall flow rivers of living water."[9]

C.W. Leadbeater, one of the first who—stimulated by Arthur Avalon's book *The Serpent Power*[10]—published a book about the chakras in the twentieth century, sees the situation of the crown chakra symbolized in the twenty-four elders of the Revelation of St. John, who lay down their crowns before God as they worship Him.[11] He writes: "In a highly developed man, this coronal chakra pours out a splendour and glory which makes for him a veritable crown; and the meaning of that passage of scripture is that all that he has gained, all the magnificent karma that he makes, all the wondrous spiritual force that he generates— all *that* he casts perpetually at the feet of the Logos to be used in His work. So over and over again can he continue to cast down his golden crown, because it continually re-forms as the force wells up from within him."[12]

Exercise to Develop the Crown Chakra

- Place your hands together in front of your chest and then slowly stretch them as far upward as you can (see figure 30, page 90). While you do this, think or speak, "I am in God."

- Then lower your hands slowly to the top of your head and form a crown by slightly opening the hands. Either think or speak, "God is in me."

- Stay in this position for a moment and then return to your starting position. Repeat this exercise as often as it feels right to you.

Figure 30.   The first four poses.

If you do the seven physical exercises for the individual chakras one after the other, then you can conclude with the "lemniscate" (see figure 31, page 91). Start the movement by moving toward the right shoulder.

- As you do the lemniscate, think or speak:

  1. "The eternal God"

  2. "Who is our mother . . ."

  3. "And our father . . ."

  4. "Blesses us and all creatures . . ."

[The number stands for the respective exercise unit.]

- Now do the exercise in the opposite direction by starting the movement toward the left shoulder. As you do this, think or speak:

  5. "... As it was in the beginning ..."

  6. "Now and forevermore ..."

  7. "And from eternity ..."

  8. "... To eternity."

- Then place your hands on your chest (right hand on top of the left). As you do this, think or speak, "Amen."

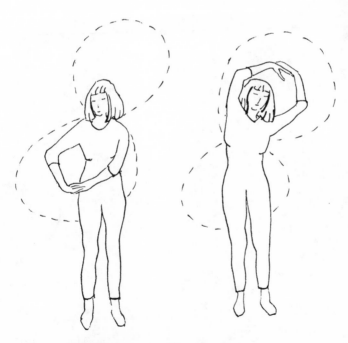

Figure 31.   The lemniscate.

Part III

The Chakras and Color

The Symbolic Colors
of the Chakras

In connection with the chakras, we encounter colors in four different ways: the natural colors, the ancient East Indian colors, the colors of the rainbow, and the colors of the personal chakras. We shall discuss them all in detail in the following text.

1. *Natural Colors:* People who have the ability to see the chakras see them—similar to the aura (which can be made visible with the help of Kirlian photography)—in constantly changing colors, depending on the emotional/physical state of the respective person.[1]

2. *Ancient East Indian Colors:* In his book *The Serpent Power*, Arthur Avalon shows the ancient East-Indian chakra symbols in color, but these illustrations are dated now. The various colors express the liveliness of the individual chakras and highlight the detailed meaning of the individual chakra symbols in a way that is not always clearly understandable to the Western observer.[2]

3. *The Rainbow Colors:* The seven rainbow colors were first identified as red-orange-yellow-green-blue-indigo-violet, the primary colors of human vision, in the eighteenth century by Isaac Newton. (Orange and indigo had previously been missing from this

list.) These colors are associated with the individual chakras and respectively interpreted in psychological terms. We call these seven colors the psychological primary colors of the chakras. They have proved themselves in the chakra meditation, so only these rainbow colors will be discussed in the following sections.

4. *The Personal Chakra Colors:* During chakra meditations, people have often imagined the seven primary colors in a different order, or even in different colors. When this occurs, the psychic level symbolized by this respective chakra can, in turn, be accordingly illuminated by this color (in a way similar to the personal chakra animals).[3]

Red—
the Root Chakra

In Hebrew, the words *red, blood, earth,* and *human being* have the same linguistic root. In other languages, red is the basic primary color and therefore means not only "red," but also "color" and "colorful." For the color red, we differentiate between bright, flashy red, and subdued, quiet red. Bright red is a centrifugal red, and the subdued is the centripetal red. The first color is extroverted (oriented toward the outside) red, and the second is introverted (oriented toward the inside) red. Extroverted red is psychologically (not biologically!) "masculine," and introverted red is psychologically "feminine." Bright red symbolizes life that has an effect in the outside world, and subdued red symbolizes the concealed, inner life. Red directed toward the outside is the expression of strong emotions (love, hate): it is the red of Mars. This outwardly directed red also means death, because blood flowing outward causes death, while inner blood indicates life.

In the color red, we also encounter other contrasts. For example, the Devil is portrayed in red as a symbol of one-sidedness while alchemy uses the red of *rubedo* to symbolize the highest developmental level of the union of opposites. So there is an enormous tension in red: love and hate, life and death, one-sidedness and wholeness. In this range of meaning, red is the corresponding color for Earth and for the root chakra in which everything is contained, but not yet developed.

Red also represents energy and strength. It is therefore an appropriate expression for the power of kundalini that rests in Muladhara. When someone "sees red," then he or she can develop virtually superhuman powers. I once experienced this in an alarmingly impressive way at a psychiatric clinic. A middle-aged man, who I had experienced as peaceful up to that point, one day went on a rampage and smashed everything with tremendous strength. He even shattered a well-secured door. I later talked to him and asked how such an outburst could happen. He said, "Suddenly, everything was red: the chairs, the table, the walls, the shelves, the windows, and the doors. Everything was totally red. A very strong power flared up inside me. And without particularly exerting myself, I smashed everything that got in my way. I simply had to do it. It practically happened on its own."

Orange—the Polarity Chakra

Orange is a composite color. It has portions of Earth's red and the Sun's yellow. Orange stands between heavenly gold and earthy red. We visibly encounter the orange of the polarity chakra in the setting sun, which sets in shades of orange and red in the Western sea in order to begin the nighttime sea journey. The sun of consciousness and day sets to enter into the area of the unconscious and the night. With the polarity chakra, we enter the realm of the unconscious, where we encounter the counterpole to the conscious reality of everyday life and therefore the "polarity." We also find orange, as the color of polarity and the opposing tensions, in some mythical figures. For example, Helen of Troy, who had a liaison with both a Greek general and a Trojan prince, wears an orange-colored veil. The Muses, as daughters of the Heavens and Earth, are also dressed in orange. Dionysius—who symbolizes the opposites of old and young, masculine and feminine, mortal and immortal, sober and drunk—also wears an orange garment.

Among the gemstones of Heavenly Jerusalem, the hyacinth (a precious stone of the ancients, sometimes thought to be a sapphire) symbolizes the polarity of earthly blood and heavenly sun.[1] Orange rules over other colors either through its positive outshining or through negative repression. According to Goethe, orange gives us "a feeling of warmth and delight," but it can also be an expression of something "unbearably violent." For example, orange is the color of the Northern Irish "Orange Order," which stands for the polarization of North Ireland.

Yellow—the Solar Plexus Chakra

The color yellow is associated with the solar plexus chakra. Like every other color, yellow is also an ambivalent color. The sun is the symbol of this ambivalence: on the one hand, it can shine as the golden sun full of joy and delight, symbolizing an invigorating power; on the other hand, it can be the glistening, burning sun that dries out the ground and brings suffering and death to plants, animals, and even human beings.

In Greek mythology, we encounter the ambivalence of yellow in the form of golden-yellow apples. These are the golden apples of the Hesperides, which the Earth Mother, Gaia, gives to Zeus and Hera, the divine couple, as their wedding gift. These apples are symbols of harmony and love. They are also the golden apples of Eris, which Paris gives to Aphrodite as "the most beautiful," which in turn triggers the Trojan War, discord, and hate.

In its psychological interpretation, yellow is connected with power, insight, intelligence, and the rational mind on the one hand, but with falseness, mistrust, betrayal, doubt, and madness on the other.

In alchemy, yellow sulfur is the "spiritual gold" and "primary mover," that "turns the wheels and the axis in a circle" according to an alchemical text—which is an illusion to the divine heavenly chariot seen by the prophet Ezekiel.[1] This heavenly chariot is an impressive image for the solar plexus chakra, which is symbolized by yellow fire and a center that turns itself. According to its psychological interpretation, it triggers and illustrates the psychic process of transformation.

In the pictorial language of the runes, yellow is connected with the sign for "walking forward."

Green—the Heart Chakra

Green is the color of growth. The old High German root, *gruoni* is still contained in the English word "grow." Growing means that something exists but has not yet developed completely. People who are beginning development are called "unripe," and sometimes disparaged as "green" or a "greenhorn." On the other hand, green is felt to be something very beautiful. In the Book of Sirach, it says, "The eye desires grace and beauty, but the green shoots of grain more than both."[1] Green is the color of the middle, where the lower yellow and upper blue unite. Garish green and the green-yellow of envy are both oriented downward.[2] An upward orientation is ascribed to "green power," which depicts the cosmos that is "interwoven with green and imbued with green" for St. Hildegard of Bingen; in her eyes, it is also the divine force that brings wholeness and healing. Accordingly, a schizophrenic reported immediately after his healing, "As the healing approached, I felt as if I were gliding into a wonderful peace. Everything was green in my room . . . I was in Paradise—in the womb of the mother."[3] (So, "seeing green" is the opposite polarity of "seeing red!")

As the color of the middle, green stands between Heaven and Earth, between above and below, between hot and cold. The green mosque in Konya is the central holy shrine of the Sufi dancing dervishes, who constantly turn around their own center and therefore symbolize the unity of all Creation.[4] In the East Indian trio of gods, green is associated with the god Vishnu, the preserver of the world.

The Christian symbol of the middle is the green cross of Christ, an archetype of hope. Medieval Christians expressed their hopes with the Latin sentence, *Crux spes unica mea* ("The cross is my only hope.") Early Christians found a concealed message regarding their profession of faith in the first and last letters of the Greek word for "green" *(Chloros): Christus Soter* ("Christ is the savior.")[5] Some folk songs praise the color green as an expression of hope, such as the German Christmas song, "O Tannenbaum" ("Oh Christmas Tree, O Christmas Tree, How are your leaves so verdant . . ." The hope and steadfastness of green gives us strength and comfort at any time.

Green is also a color of acceptance and affection (the Germanic rune for "green" means "encounter"). Green symbolizes the balancing of opposites, which creates peace.

Blue—the Throat Chakra

An East Indian myth tells us how the color blue was created, "As the world was created from the cosmic ocean, the first substance that came to the surface was the poison of the cosmic snake. The poison cannot be assimilated by humans, or angels, or demons. It also cannot be assimilated by the gods, because it is the cosmic force of destruction. There is only one being who can drink this poison, and this is the 'cosmic human' who is the existence and origin of all existence—as well as the destructive forces of the cosmos—namely, the god Shiva. When Shiva drank the poison, it constricted him and his throat turned totally blue. This is how the color blue came into being. As a result, the snake poison was transformed into *Amrita*. It became the drink of eternal life."[1]

This myth makes it clear that blue is a mysterious color. Blue was created when the poison of the snake became the gift of the gods (the German word for *gift* means "poison")—a cryptic thought that leads us directly into a symbolic meaning of the blue throat chakra.

Like all colors, blue is ambivalent. On the one hand, it stands for truth and loyalty; on the other, it represents coldness and deception ("blue with cold," "singing the blues," "talking until you are blue in the face"). However, blue is also a secretive color, because it brings surprises ("the blue moon"). Blue belongs to Virgo, the zodiac sign, and to the Virgin Mary. For the artist Kandinsky, blue expresses an "unworldly solemnity."

Indigo—the Third Eye Chakra

Indigo is a mixture of blue and violet. It still participates in the polarity of blue (which has a polarized tension to "red") and is already part of the unity of violet (in which red and blue have merged into a unity).

Indigo is an apt symbol for the coexistence of the "ego" (polarity) and the "Self" (unity). The "ego-self" axis is perfectly developed in the third eye. The will of the ego has become one with the will of the Self.

Indigo symbolizes the transition from waking to sleeping, and from sleeping to waking (which equal the hypnopompic and the hypnagogic states), from dreams to reality, and from reality to dreams. From this close proximity to the unconscious, deep insights arise that are characteristic of the third eye.

Indigo stands for meditation, mysticism, religion, and empathy. It also symbolizes the connection with cosmic intelligence and wisdom.

Violet—the Crown Chakra

Violet is the unification of red and blue, meaning the union of the first "lower" chakra (red) and the first "upper" chakra (blue). Consequently, this symbolizes the unification of the chakras in general.

Unification and unity is the theme of the crown chakra that rules above everything else. There is nothing more that can be separated or broken in two in the crown chakra. Everything is one. There is no more duality in the crown chakra, since the crown chakra is not involved with the superficial world, which is characterized by polarity. The crown chakra symbolizes the superficial and cryptic world that has become one unity. The color violet also expresses that everything is one within the crown chakra. We can illustrate this using the polarities of masculine and feminine. On the one hand, red is considered masculine, but it is also seen as feminine. The aggressive Mars red is considered masculine (in his color test, Dr. Max Luescher calls it "the expression of impulsive conquest"). On the other hand, warm, earthy red is seen as feminine. The situation is similar for blue: cool sky-blue is considered masculine, while warm intuitive blue is seen as feminine (in his color test, Luescher calls it "an expression of tender devotion"). Violet is the unity between all aspects of blue and red, which also includes masculine and feminine.

Violet also symbolizes unity between the root chakra and the crown chakra. On the one hand, violet is a symbol of the undifferentiated unity that corresponds to the root chakra (red and blue are undifferentiated together, as in a mixture). It is like the beginning of Creation, where everything is contained in one big tohubohu.[1] On the other hand, violet is the symbol of a differentiated unity that corresponds to the crown chakra. It is the unification of the developed polarity. (Ingrid Riedel calls this undifferentiated unity androgynous violet, while the differentiated unity is hermaphroditic violet.[2])

Consequently, the violet associated with the crown chakra is the unity of everything that exists, from Heaven and Earth, life and death, subject and object, "positive" and "negative," and all of the other polarities. Since all opposites are united in the crown chakra (including the opposites of "everything" and "nothing"), they lose their respective negative or positive characteristics. The valuations of positive and negative no longer exist in this unity for which duality no longer exists. All of this is symbolized by the color violet.

A Color Meditation

For a group meditation, the leader can slowly read the following text and interrupt it with pauses. If you are alone, you can read this material into a tape recorder and listen to it as you relax, sitting or lying down, and imagine the following journey.

In the early morning, you leave on a journey. Your path leads you to a field of red poppy flowers. You stop and let the red of the flowers and the red of the earth have their effect on you. The red energy flows through your body and its organs. You are practically flooded by the red of this poppy-flower field. You let yourself become enveloped in red light, which connects you with Mother Earth. Thank the earth for supporting and nourishing you, and for providing you with energy.

[Silence]

Then you continue. The view opens up as you come to a river, and you see that the orange-red sun is rising. The brilliant orange orb of the sun is reflected in the quietly flowing water. You stop and let the color orange have its effect on you. Breathe in the orange that is reflected in the water, and experience how this energy permeates and illuminates you. Your body, which consists mostly of water, absorbs this orange. Feel how this color stimulates you, and sense the powers of the water. Look into the water for a long time and let yourself become invigorated and transformed by the orange color.

[Silence]

The sun slowly rises and changes into a radiant yellow. Continue to walk toward a luminous yellow field of sunflowers. Absorb this yellow light and inhale it deeply. Your solar plexus opens wide at the sight of the yellow flowers that are related to it. Like a cleansing fire, the yellow energy blazes through your body with all its feelings and emotions. Consciously expose yourself to the yellow light of the sun and the flowers. The golden sunlight becomes warmer and reminds you of the fire found in the inner life processes.

[Silence]

The path now leads you to a hill. Walk through a green meadow to the edge of the forest. Stop under the green canopy of a beech tree. The hanging branches, with their delicate green leaves, surround you like a tent. The wind whispers quietly through the leaves. Let it gently blow through you. Your heart opens wide and absorbs the green.

[Silence]

Then walk further up the mountain. A blue sky arches above you. Lay down on your back and let yourself be enveloped and illuminated by the blue of the heavens. In this heavenly blue, you encounter an otherworldly reality that penetrates your earthly existence in a healing way.

[Silence]

You continue to walk, and then you see yourself standing in front of a chapel. You enter it and stop in the anteroom. Indigo-blue panes of glass give the room an atmosphere of peace. Breathe in this indigo-blue light. The indigo-blue calms your mind and awakens a premonition of the divine world within you. Let yourself be imbued with the energy of this color.

[Silence]

Go inside the chapel. The sun shines through the violet windowpanes. There is a wonderful violet amethyst on the altar. Let yourself be flooded by the violet light. Inhale it with your breath and feel how the violet penetrates your entire being. You would like to stay here. Everything is very quiet, and everything within you is silent. You have arrived. You are here. You have entered into divine being.

[Silence]

Once again, absorb the violet light into your body. Then leave through the indigo-blue illuminated anteroom and look outside at the blue sky. Slowly climb down the mountain, seeing the green roof of beech leaves above you.

Leave the forest and look at the yellow field of sunflowers. Stop at the river and look into the water, which is colored a brilliant orange by the setting sun. Then keep on walking. See the poppy flowers glow in the evening light. You now leave this wonderful inner reality.

Move a little and open your eyes. Notice the outer, visible reality. Do one of the harmonization exercises (see pages 26–29) and return to the reality of everyday life.

Part IV

The Chakras and Inner Animals

The Personal Chakra Animals

"I experienced something strange today," said a 30-year-old woman, as we began to talk. "I *dreamed* of an eagle, and then I woke up and noticed that I not only dreamed of an eagle but that I *was* an eagle. I had wings instead of arms and hands; I felt how my tendons stretched, and how I could powerfully move my wings. My body was feathered, and instead of feet, I had claws. Instead of a mouth, I felt a powerful, curved beak, and my eyes could see much more sharply than otherwise. I could even recognize details at great distances. I *was* an eagle!"

While this woman told me of her experience, it reminded me of the fairy tale of the seven ravens and other tales in which people are changed into animals. However, I also thought of the Native American shamans I have met who have had very similar experiences. They described these experiences to me in such real terms that I didn't know whether they were actually transformed into animals, or whether this was an extremely realistic inner experience. I also thought about a woman, who lived in a Swiss village, who always wore a scarf on her head because she was missing one ear. She supposedly had the ability to change herself into a rabbit. While in this state, they say, a hunter shot off one of her ears.

I also encounter animals in my own dreams, and in the dreams that other people tell me about. In these dreams, there are cats, dogs, frogs, snakes, elephants, bears, horses, tigers, lions, scorpions, foxes, rabbits, fish, birds, insects, reptiles—every kind of animal that creeps and flies.

When I dream of an animal myself, or even sometimes of being an animal, I sometimes try to feel like this animal when I wake up. When I do this, I am always amazed that it is actually possible to experience myself as a bear or an eagle, or even as a whale or snake.

I once experienced quite impressively that this is not just a game, but that these animals—as in the fairy tales—can be inner helpers: I attended a shamanism course that involved going into the alpha state (meaning a state between waking and sleeping) to the muffled sounds of a shaman's drum and then imagining an animal. Since I have always preferred eagles because of my first name (Ar-nold means "the one who rules the eagles"), I thought that I would imagine an eagle. However, to my surprise, a big, portly brown bear emerged from inside of me. I was a bear during this entire course and, above all, experienced the lazy and comfortable aspect of this bear. This state continued even after the conclusion of the course when I attended a meeting in which I was to be nominated for an honorable board position. My ambitious eagle side thought this position was quite desirable, but I was still living too much in my lazy bear aspect and therefore declined.

Afterward, I was quite annoyed at what I had done. I was angry at "this stupid bear fantasy" that had ruined the position on the board for me. Yet, a few weeks later I noticed the exertion, in terms of time and energy, that this position would have cost me. I was very happy that I had refused it. Even today, I am thankful to my nice, comfortable, and lazy bear for protecting me against making the wrong decision.

We also encounter animals in the chakra symbols, such as the elephant in the root chakra, the Leviathan in the po-

larity chakra, the ram in the solar plexus chakra, the antelope in the heart chakra and, once again, the elephant in the
throat chakra. These animals characterize the psychological
meaning of the individual chakras. The four lower animals
also personify the elements—earth, water, fire, and air.

Animals are also used in astrology to symbolize the
elements. The bull (Taurus) embodies earth, the eagle (or
scorpion/dragon = Scorpio), water, the lion (Leo) represents
fire, and the human being (Aquarius), air. (The human
being is considered an animal in this case.)

In the Bible, these elemental animals are the divine
guardians of the throne and the archetypes of the cosmos.[1]
Animals therefore belong directly to God; they share in
God's holiness.

We encounter animals in our dreams, in our imagination, in the chakra symbols, in astrology (where the entire
year is described as an animal cycle: *zodiac* in Greek) and in
the four biblical animals that are identical to the elemental
animals of the zodiac.

While the animals of the chakra symbols are associated
with a specific chakra, making them the objective represen-
tative of the respective chakras, the animals in our dreams
and imagination have a subjective character. These are our
very personal animals. In the 1980s, the American psychol-
ogist E. S. Galegos connected the chakras with personal
chakra animals instead of the traditional chakra animals.[2]

Working with personal chakra animals makes sense because the situation is very similar when we apply it to astrology or the chakra colors. In addition to the ideal (or natural)
horoscope, there is a personal horoscope. This involves using
the symbolism of the natural zodiac to confront the personal
horoscope, which is calculated for the actual time and place
of birth, and the starting point of our path of individuation.[3]

There are also personal colors—which, when compared with the colors of the rainbow provide us with information about the current state of the respective chakras—in addition to the "natural" colors of the chakras. We can use the background of the ideal or "natural" chakra animals to explore our personal chakra animals. When, for example, we encounter a nightingale instead of an elephant in the root chakra, then we probably should question our relationship to the earth elements and how we are rooted in the reality of this world.

When I began to encourage other people to encounter their own personal chakra animals, I was very surprised. Each of them—without an exception—responded very positively to this approach to the unconscious. I quickly noticed that we do not even have to imagine these animals, since they are already here, and show themselves as soon as we become interested in them.

If we involve ourselves with these animals over a certain portion of our path, we will notice that these personal chakra animals are not meaningless images of our imagination, but inner helpers who tell us something about the state of the inner regions in which we imagine them. If there appears to be a problem with any one of these animals, then we can put ourselves in their place, connecting it with the other personal chakra animals. We can then experience how this brings change and healing.

Galegos cites several interesting examples. One example mentions a woman who had a strained and tense voice. She imagined a mouse in her throat chakra. When this woman asked the mouse what it needed, the mouse said that its hole was too small, could she possibly make it a little bigger? In her imagination, the woman succeeded in stretching the hole, and her voice became fuller and deeper.[4]

When imagining, it is important to simply let the animals come, without influencing the imagination through wishful thinking. Every animal that comes voluntarily is important, even if we don't understand it immediately. If a "phony" animal should appear at some point, we don't have to worry about it. It will disappear soon and make room for a "genuine" animal.

Occasionally, an object instead of an animal may emerge from our unconscious. For example, a 12-year-old boy imagined a fork and spoon. When his teacher, who did the imagination exercise with the student, asked him what happens next with the fork and spoon, the boy answered: "I use them to roll up the rainbow—like spaghetti—so that I can eat it."[5]

This imagination exercise makes it clear that the boy was in the process of internalizing the rainbow (a symbol of psychic wholeness) in order to find the appropriate balance of body, mind, and soul for his age.

Encountering Your Animals

How can you encounter your personal chakra animals? Here is a suggestion:

- Sit or lie down comfortably. (If you do this imagination exercise in a group, you can put yourself into an alpha state using a relaxation exercise or by listening to a muffled drum.)

- Direct your attention to your root chakra and ask the animal that lives there to show itself. Give this animal plenty of time. (Some animals are shy and only gradually reveal themselves.) Attentively observe the behavior of this animal.

- Make contact with the animal and ask it what it needs.

- In your imagination, try to give the animal what it needs.

- Ask the animal if it would like to give you something that you need.

- If the animal gives you something, accept it with gratitude.

- If you have no more questions to ask, say good-bye to your animal.

- Continue on to the next chakra and ask the animal that lives there to show itself. Use the same approach as you did for the root chakra for the second and other chakras. (The order doesn't have to be rigid. You can, for example, also begin with the solar plexus chakra and continue to the polarity and the root chakra. However, you should generally begin with the lower chakras.)

- When you have reached the crown chakra, once again remember all seven chakra animals and thank them for making contact with you.

Taking these inner animals seriously can give your life a new quality. C. G. Jung said: "If every individual had a better relationship to the animals within him, he would also set a higher value on life."[6]

The Healing Circle

Sometimes an animal may live in an unusual place (a bird living in the root chakra, or a horse in the crown chakra), or it may behave in an unusual way (such as being handicapped, sick, fearful, or aggressive), or problems cannot be cleared up in the conversation with the animal. If this is the case, then ask each of the animals individually if it is willing to form a healing circle, and whether this is the right time for such a meeting.

If the animals agree to do so, ask the animal in the crown chakra if it is ready to call such a meeting.

If the crown-chakra animal agrees to this, let it determine the place where this meeting should take place and invite all the other animals to it.

Observe the animals as they come to the meeting place. Watch to see how they form the circle, and who sits or lays next to whom in this circle. (Some animals prefer a place on a tree.)

You are also present in the circle. Where is your place? Who sits next to you? Who sits across from you? Welcome all the animals. Thank them for coming and for allowing you to be a part of the circle.

Now tell the animals what you are concerned about (for example: "Wolf, I'm afraid of you!" or, "Nightingale, it bothers me that you live in my root chakra!") and then wait for a response from the respective animal and from the other animals. Let the animals talk and take action. It is often quite astonishing to learn how wise these animals are and how they solve problems that we cannot solve.

In case you have the impression that the animals are doing something wrong, tell them this. If one animal wants to harm (or eat) you, do not permit this. Although the animals are often wiser than we are, and can often help where we cannot help, they are not the rulers in our house. They are the inner helpers. We hold the scepter in our hands. However, we need our authority only when the animals want to harm us (which is very rarely the case). Aggressive animals are frequently transformed into helpful animals during (or after) the meeting of the healing circle.

If there are no more questions, thank the animals and let them go in peace.

Part V

The Chakras in Western Interpretation

The Path of the Chakras in the Bible

When the New Testament says that Jesus is an "example" for us, and that we can walk "in his footsteps,"[1] it expresses the idea that the Jesus path is the archetype for our own.

C. G. Jung says it in these words: "Christ lived a concrete, personal, and unique life, which, in all essential features had at the same time an archetypal character. . . . Since the life of Christ is archetypal to a high degree, it represents to just that degree the life of the archetype. But since the archetype is the unconscious precondition of every human life, its life, when revealed, also reveals the hidden unconscious ground-life of every individual. That is to say, what happens in the life of Christ happens always and everywhere. In the Christian archetype, all lives of this kind are prefigured and are expressed over and over."[2] So the path of Jesus is the archetype for our path, and also the archetype for the process of individuation, as it is reflected in the chakra symbols. The chakras are not only the "memory aids" for the path of individuation given to our body, but also the path of Jesus.

The Root Chakra reminds us of the fact that Jesus was totally human, with all the normal physical and emotional impulses, and all the family and social ties.

The Polarity Chakra reminds us that Jesus was also aware of the powers of the unconscious. He knew that "evil" thoughts come from the "heart" (which means the unconscious mind)[3] and penetrate into consciousness.[4]

The Solar Plexus Chakra reminds us of Jesus' confrontation with the temptations that plagued him and tried to divert him from the path that had been traced out for him.[5]

The Heart Chakra reminds us that Jesus overcame these temptations over and over, bringing together the feuding inner forces into a *coniuntio-oppositorium* ("union of opposites") as a dynamic polarity.

The Throat Chakra reminds us that Jesus' words[6] and deeds,[7] are the earthly temporality that reflect the eternal heavenly realm.

The Third Eye Chakra reminds us that Jesus constantly listened to his inner voice in order to perceive and carry out the will of his true self ("the will of God").

The Crown Chakra reminds us that Jesus brought all of the experience of his earthly life into "heaven" and thereby united himself with the divine. In chakra meditation, we can personally experience these stages of Jesus' path.[8] The following meditation provides the instructions for this approach.

ROOT CHAKRA: ROOTED IN EARTH

Direct your attention to your root chakra and remind yourself that it is a symbol of your rootedness on Earth and in the world.

Just like you, Jesus was also rooted on Earth and in the world. He lived at a certain time in a specific country. He belonged to a certain family and a specific people. He had ancestors, relatives, and friends; he went to school and learned a trade. Just like you, Jesus encountered the joys and difficulties of everyday life. Some people understood him, and some misunderstood him. The world in which Jesus lived was a world full of possibilities that wanted to be taken advantage of and lived day by day.

In the same way as Jesus, you are also concerned with fulfilling the task that corresponds to your possibilities and abilities, contributing to shaping and preserving Earth as a result.

Root Chakra Meditation

Direct your attention to the root chakra and imagine it opening up like a flower. Red light flows into you through the opened chakra. Think or speak: "Like Jesus, I am rooted in the earth."

[Silence]

POLARITY CHAKRA: STRETCHED BETWEEN THE POLARITIES

Direct your attention to the polarity chakra and remind yourself that it is the symbol for how we human beings are stretched between the polarities. Jesus also experienced the world in which he lived as a conflicting world. Even as a 12-year-old boy, he experienced that in addition to the external voice of his parents, who expected him to obey, an inner voice exists that is superior to the outer voice. Just like you, Jesus experienced the conflict between what other people expected of him and what God called him to do.

When he was baptized, Jesus also experienced God as a conflicting God. He experienced him as the light God who said to him, "Thou art my beloved son; in whom I am well pleased" (Mark 1:11), and as the dark God who drove him out into the wilderness so that Satan could tempt him.[9]

Jesus also experienced this conflict within himself. It is written that he was made—just like you and me—"in the likeness of sinful flesh" (Romans 8:3). This means that he is aware of the powers of the unconscious and—just like you and me—is stretched between the polarities.

Polarity Chakra Meditation

Direct your attention to the polarity chakra and imagine it opening up like a flower. Orange light streams into you through the opened chakra. Think or speak: "Like Jesus, I am stretched between the two polarities."

[Silence]

SOLAR PLEXUS CHAKRA: UNITING THE OPPOSITES

Direct your attention to your solar plexus chakra and remind yourself that it is a symbol for the process of uniting the opposites. Jesus "has been tempted as we are" (Hebrews 4:15). He knows, as you and I do, how to adapt himself to the temptation and take the path of least resistance. He resists this temptation and takes his own path, the path that had been drawn for him.

But Jesus also knows, as you and I do, the temptation of one-sidedness, of declaring loyalty to one group or the other, and fighting the opposing party. Yet, Jesus also resists this temptation and takes his own path by reconciling the poles within himself, therefore contributing to the reconciliation of the polarities in his surrounding world.[10]

Solar Plexus Chakra Meditation

Direct your attention to your solar plexus chakra and imagine it opening up like a flower. Yellow light flows into you through the opened chakra. Think or speak: "Like Jesus, I resist the temptation to adapt and to be one-sided."

[Silence]

HEART CHAKRA: EXPERIENCING PEACE

Direct your attention to the heart chakra and remind yourself that it is a symbol for peace as the dynamic polarity.

Because Jesus resists the temptation to adapt and to polarize, he unites the opposite poles into a dynamic polarity. "Peace" is not at all related to the abstract "calm," but is an energy that is characterized by the tension-charged equilibrium of the poles.[11] Jesus stands above the poles of thinking and feeling, sensation and intuition, extroverted and introverted, masculine and feminine, poor and rich, being hungry and being full, pain and well-being, love and anger, sadness and happiness, suffering and joy, living and dying. Peace as a polar dynamic rules in his heart. You and I can also experience this peace as often as it is possible to unite the opposites within. Then the peace of God rules in our hearts as well.

Heart Chakra Meditation

Direct your attention to the heart chakra and imagine it opening up like a flower. Green light flows into you through the opened chakra. Think or speak: "As in Jesus' heart, the peace of God also reigns in my heart."

[Silence]

THROAT CHAKRA: ENCOUNTERING THE SYMBOL

Direct your attention to the throat chakra and remind yourself that it is a symbol for the interrelation of the reality of this world and the otherworldly reality.

For Jesus, the various manifestations of this earthly world were metaphors for the other, heavenly world. Jesus himself is the archetype for the coexistence and relationship between human and divine reality. He is completely human and is a part of everything earthly and human. But he is also completely "God," and is part of everything divine and heavenly. By letting this Christ reality have an effect on you and increasingly perceiving it in everything earthly, you will be "changed into the same image from glory to glory even as by the spirit of the Lord" (II Corinthians 3:18).

Throat Chakra Meditation

Direct your attention to the throat chakra and imagine it opening up like a flower. Blue light flows into you through the opened chakra. Think or speak: "According to the example of Jesus, I find the heavenly within the earthly."

[Silence]

THIRD EYE CHAKRA:
BECOMING ONE WITH THE INNER WILL

Direct your attention to the third eye and remind yourself that it is a symbol for your inner will becoming one with the divine will.

Jesus' life was characterized by his striving for harmony between his will and divine will. It was therefore possible for him to say, "My meat is to do the will of him that sent me, and to finish his work" (John 4:34). Or, "For I came down from heaven not to do mine own will, but the will of him that sent me" (John 6:38). The work of Jesus is therefore acting in harmony with the voice of his true Self, meaning the voice of God.

And how can we reach a harmonious state between the will of our ego and the will of God (our true Self)? In prayer. The person who prays struggles with God in prayer and is victorious when God within him has triumphed. How extreme such a "struggle with God" can be is shown by Jesus' prayer struggle at Gethsemane. Here as well, Jesus was completely human.

Third Eye Chakra Meditation

Direct your attention to the third eye and imagine it opening up like a flower. Indigo-blue light flows into you through the opened chakra. Think or speak: "Like Jesus, I follow my inner voice."

[Silence]

CROWN CHAKRA: UNION WITH GOD

Direct your attention to the crown chakra and remind yourself that it is a symbol for union with God. An expression of union with God is the ascension of Jesus into Heaven. Jesus brought everything into Heaven that he had incorporated into himself during his life on Earth and his descent into the underworld. The ascension into Heaven is the countermovement to his act of becoming human. When he became human, Jesus brought Heaven to Earth; when he ascended to Heaven, he took the transformed Earth back to Heaven with him.

In connection with the living Christ within you, you can also descend into your own depths and bring everything that has been split off and suppressed to the light of day, which will allow you to find your own wholeness. The risen Christ lives in each of us as the archetype of our own true Self. With him, we are united in God.

Crown Chakra Meditation

Direct your attention to the crown chakra and imagine it opening up like a flower. Violet light flows into you through the opened chakra. Think or say: "Like Jesus, I live and work in God."

[Silence]

The Lord's Prayer
as a Chakra Meditation

In my book on the Lord's Prayer as experienced in the light of depth psychology and chakra meditation, I give a detailed description of how I discovered the Lord's Prayer Chakra Meditation. Many years have passed since then. In the meantime, countless people have discovered a new approach to the Lord's Prayer through this book and their own experiences with the Lord's Prayer Chakra Meditation. They have learned to understand it, love it, and pray it in a new way. Because of this, the Lord's Prayer Chakra Meditation has also been included here.

Jesus taught this prayer to the people who encountered God in a new way through his message. These were people who were rooted in this world and lived with wide-awake senses in the reality of everyday life. As fishermen and farmers, housewives and partners, as freedom fighters and collaborators, they lived in a world that valued whatever "stood firm." (This is the meaning of "Amen.") And so they prayed, "Amen."

In the middle of this AMEN world, in the middle of everyday life, God spoke to them through Jesus and shook them to the core. In the encounter with Jesus, they saw their lives in a new light. They recognized their one-sidedness and lack of redemption; despite their competence in professional life, they recognized that they were "sinners" who fell short of the goal of their lives.[1] In the depths of their soul, they so longed for redemption that they cried out to God, "Deliver us from evil."

They were people who set out to follow Jesus. In the process, they discovered that this was not a simple path, but that they were repeatedly confronted with temptations. They also experienced the threat of succumbing to these temptations.[2] And so they begged God, "Lead us not into temptation."

But in the presence of Jesus, they experienced that God forgave them their shortcomings over and over, and they also learned to forgive others.[3] So they repeatedly prayed anew to God: "Forgive us our debts as we forgive our debtors."

In the presence of Jesus, they also had the experience of never lacking in worldly goods.[4] God provided enough bread to satisfy the hunger of the masses.[5] For them, earthly bread became a metaphor for the heavenly bread that their soul needed, in the same way that their bodies required earthly bread.[6] And they prayed: "Give us this day our daily bread," meaning both earthly and heavenly "bread."[7]

In the presence of Jesus, the longing for the kingdom of God, of which Jesus spoke time and again, awoke within them. They recognized that the kingdom of God dawned wherever the will of God occurred. And so they prayed: "Thy Kingdom come—Thy will be done, on Earth as it is in Heaven."

In the presence of Jesus, they ultimately became familiar with God in a new way. They learned to trust him like a loving father. But they also realized that God is not just the "Abba" ("Papa"), who is devoted in a friendly way and allows them to experience "Heaven" in everyday life. He is also a very different God, who rules the cosmos, causing the angels to cover their faces at the sight of his holiness. They realized that this God cannot be compared and equated with any type of earthly experience, but that his "name" is above all other names and is unspeakable. And so they prayed to God: "Our Father who art in Heaven—hallowed be Thy name."

As already mentioned, Jesus taught this prayer to the people who had experiences of God and themselves in the encounter with him. Consequently, they could pray in retrospect[8]:

> *Our Father who art in heaven,*
> *Hallowed be thy name.*
> *Thy kingdom come*
> *Thy will be done*
> *On earth as it is in heaven.*
> *Give us this day our daily bread;*
> *And forgive us our debts*
> *As we also have forgiven our debtors;*
> *And lead us not into temptation*
> *But deliver us from evil.*
> *Amen.*

However, over the course of centuries, this prayer has been "prayed" by many people who did not have the personal experiences of faith upon which its message is based. As a result, the prayer has become a formula (sometimes even a magical one) that is just recited monotonously. Even people who had set out on the path to encounter God and themselves became estranged from it. In the Lord's Prayer Chakra Meditation, people can encounter Jesus' prayer in a completely new way. The individual statements of the Lord's Prayer—beginning with the AMEN—can become reminders and memory aids for the path you have taken, and are still taking, in the process of becoming whole. In the Lord's Prayer Chakra Meditation, you can experience the stages of your path to God and to yourself. The following text offers ideas and help for doing the meditation.

THE LORD'S PRAYER CHAKRA MEDITATION

Root Chakra: *AMEN*

> *You live in this world.*
> *You live right now in this moment.*
> *You live on Earth.*
> *It is your mother.*
> *You feel that the Earth supports you.*
> *You are firmly rooted in Earth*
> *Right where you are.*
> *You tackle the task*
> *That is now laid at your feet.*

Direct your attention to the root chakra and imagine it opening like a flower. Red light streams into you through the opened chakra. As you do this, think or speak,

> *"AMEN."*

Polarity Chakra: *Deliver Us from Evil*

> *You live in a divided world.*
> *You separate yourself*
> *From people who threaten you.*
> *But you are also threatened*
> *By your own shadow.*
> *You know that such polarizations*
> *Are evil.*
> *You therefore long for redemption*
> *From this divided state.*
> *You long for wholeness.*

Direct your attention to the polarity chakra and imagine it opening up like a flower. Orange light streams into you through the opened chakra. As you do this, ask God:

> *"Deliver us from evil."*

Solar Plexus Chakra: *Lead Us Not into Temptation*

> *Opening up to the spirit of God means*
> *Saying "yes" to change.*
> *Over and over you are faced with the*
>   *temptation*
> *Of clinging to one-sidedness*
> *Instead of finding a golden mean;*
> *Or clinging to whatever is old but outdated*
> *Instead of letting it go to its death*
> *So that something new can be created.*

Direct your attention to the solar plexus chakra and imagine that it is opening up like a flower. Yellow light streams into you through the opened chakra. As you do this, ask God:

> *"Lead us not into temptation."*

Heart Chakra: *Forgive Us Our Debts*
As We Forgive Our Debtors

> *Now think of situations in which you*
> *Missed the goal of your life,*
> *Where you gave in to temptations,*

Where were untrue to yourself,
Where you said "no" to impulses
from your true Self.
Bring these failed goals to the cross of
Christ.
The cross is a symbol of wholeness.
The "yes" and the "no" have become
united in the cross.
All the failed goals,
both your own and those of others,
have been rescinded in the cross.

Direct your attention to the heart chakra and imagine that
it is opening like a flower. Green light streams into you
through the opened chakra. As you do this, ask God:

"Forgive us our debts
As we forgive our debtors."

Throat Chakra: *Give Us This Day Our Daily Bread*

Everyone lives from the earthly bread.
You and all people are connected to
Mother Earth
And all of her children
Through earthly bread.
All earthly bread
Is an archetype of the heavenly bread
That nourishes the inner person.
Through it, you are connected
With all human beings
Who open themselves for the spirit of God.

Direct your attention to the throat chakra and imagine that it is opening up like a flower. Blue light streams into you through the opened chakra. As you do this, ask God:

>"Give us this day our daily bread."

Third Eye Chakra: *Thy will be done on Earth as it is in Heaven. Thy Kingdom Come.*

>*Your eyes are captured*
>*By the visible reality.*
>*However, you still know*
>*That the authentic reality*
>*Is invisible to the outer eyes.*
>*You therefore open your inner eye*
>*So that you can perceive the will of God*
>*And see the kingdom of God.*

Direct your attention to the third eye and imagine that it is opening up like a flower. Indigo-blue light streams into you through the opened chakra. As you do this, ask God:

>"Thy will be done on Earth as it is in
>   Heaven:
>Thy Kingdom Come."

Crown Chakra: *Our Father who art in Heaven, Hallowed be Thy name*

>*Within God*
>*Is everything:*

The Earth and sky
The mother and father
The feminine and masculine
The dark and light
By being connected with God
You are part of his wholeness
This makes his name holy.

Direct your attention to the crown chakra and imagine that it is opening up like a flower. Violet light streams into you through the opened chakra. As you do this, pray to God:

"Hallowed be Thy name
Our Father who art in Heaven."

You can finish the Lord's Prayer Chakra Meditation by making the sign of the cross. Symbolically make the longitudinal beam with your hand and speak the words:

"Thine is the kingdom"
    [hand at the level of your head],
"and the power"
    [move the hand from your head to
    the level of the root chakra],
"and the glory"
    [touch one shoulder],
"Forever and ever"
    [touch the other shoulder].
"Amen"
    [place your hand on your heart].

After you have used the Lord's Prayer Chakra Meditation to meditatively incorporate the individual phases of
your path to wholeness and call them to mind, you can now
"retrospectively" pray or sing the Lord's Prayer in the accus-
tomed manner and experience its power in a new way.
When we hold introductory courses on the Lord's Prayer
Chakra Meditation,[9] we sing the prayer using the melody
shown on pages 142–143. This melody has been adapted
from the music of Rimski-Korsakov by Maxim Kovalevski.

Und füh - re uns nicht in Ver - su - chung, son - dern er - lö -
And lead us not in to temptation, But deliver us

se uns von dem Bö - sen. Denn dein ist das Reich und die Kraft
from evil For thine is the Kingdom and

und die Herr - lich - keit in E - wig - keit. A - men.
the power and the glory forever Amen.

Chakra Symbolism in
Fairy Tales

The seven developmental phases reflected in the symbolism of the chakras are also recognized in some popular fairy tales. However, fairy tales clearly demonstrate that the development of the soul does not occur in a straight line; instead, it has more of a spiral pattern. Consequently, a "higher" phase of consciousness may already flare up during a "lower" phase of consciousness in the process of developing the soul.

ROOT CHAKRA:
DEVELOPMENTAL POSSIBILITIES

The archetypal symbol for any development is the paradise in which everything is together in oneness: God, human being, animal, plant, and mineral kingdom. Everything is together here, but not yet developed. In fairy tales, a disruptive factor enters into this "intact" world that sets the situation in motion. This state is particularly clear in fairy tales that tell of "forbidden" rooms to which entry is prohibited. Yet, the hero or heroine of the fairy tale always enters this room. They violate the prohibition. And what do they find in these forbidden rooms? For example: the picture of a beautiful princess,[1] a destructive picture of a man,[2] a black woman who turns white,[3] the triune God,[4] or the Devil.[5] Looking into the forbidden room always brings unrest and suffering with it, but it is also the beginning of a development that ends with an enormous gain.

Our unconscious has many rooms that we must enter, and of which we must take possession.[6] The more closed rooms we open, the better acquainted we become with ourselves, the more conscious and rich our life becomes. In this process, it is important to explore the numinous and fear-producing contents of the forbidden rooms because they are not compatible with our previous conscious attitude. They offer special possibilities of expanding our consciousness.

There are three ways of behaving toward forbidden rooms. First, we don't open the room. This means that everything stays the way it is. We may, perhaps, remain well behaved and adjusted, but lifeless. Second, we carefully open the door, look inside, but don't enter. This would mean that we do not become involved with the contents we see in this room, even though we know that something like this exists within us. Instead, we close the door and lead a two-faced life in the future. In terms of relationships, this means that we may know more than we are telling, but don't touch upon it. Such behavior is the death of a genuine relationship.

The third possibility is the one chosen in the fairy tales: we enter this room and become familiar with the contents of the forbidden room, letting them have their effect upon us. This sets our lives in motion.

There are closed rooms within all of us. There is a voice within that says we are not allowed to open these rooms because this would bring misfortune, or our lives would be thrown into confusion. However, there is another voice within that says that we must open these doors. As we know, prohibitions are an effective method of prompting us to transgress against them. This reminds us of the story of the Fall of Man, in which the forbidden tree is attractive because it is forbidden. It is often necessary to transgress against such a prohibition in order to become autonomous. The forbidden rooms in fairy tales are unlived possibilities. We fear them and therefore suppress them. Quite frequently, these rooms contain values from the pre-Christian era (for example: a feminine image of God or the dark aspect of God) that would enrich our lives if we could meaningfully integrate it.

POLARITY CHAKRA:
ENCOUNTER WITH OPPOSITES

Leaving paradise means encountering polarity. Many fairy tales tell us about the unequal sisters, brothers, or companions on the path, such as the Golden Maiden and the Dirty Maiden,[7] the modest and the arrogant sisters,[8] the know-it-alls and fools,[9] and many other "good" and "bad" companions.[10] We tend to identify with the good figure and reject the bad one. But the "dark" figure is also a part of us. It is good for the soul when we acknowledge the dark side and take our entire psyche seriously as a result. When we read the fairy tale, we can ask ourselves: "Where is my lazy and sassy Dirty Maiden side?" "Where is my arrogant, sadistic, scheming stepsister?" "Or where is my dark brother?" Our soul comes to life again when we accept its dark side as part of ourselves, thereby giving it the possibility of changing.

SOLAR PLEXUS CHAKRA:
UNITING OPPOSITES

When we become familiar with the world of opposites, a double temptation arises: the temptation of returning to the "world of paradise" found in the root chakra, or the temptation of getting stuck in the one-sidedness of the polarity chakra.[11] We find the temptation of returning to the world of "paradise," that is misunderstood as a land of milk and honey, in such fairy tales where the older brothers get stuck in a comfortable inn, or there is a constantly set table, or a made bed that invites the main character to stay.[12]

The temptation to be one-sided is also found in one fairy tale where the man wants to remain in poverty and doesn't take advantage of the opportunity that life (the flounder) is offering him.[13] On the other hand, his wife is fascinated by the polarity and wants more and more, until she finally wants to become like God. They both missed the point of finding the golden mean—an appropriate place to live and work that is meaningful for each individual.

Another example of one-sidedness is the prince who wants to have the golden cage, as well as the golden bird, and the golden saddle, as well as the golden horse.[14] This fairy tale also concerns finding the proper form of moderation and a happy medium. It involves connecting the opposites rather than going from one extreme to the other. Modesty is a part of wealth since wealth otherwise becomes our downfall. The precious and the simple belong together. This is why a wooden cage belongs with the golden bird and a wooden saddle with the golden horse.

The spiritual and the earthly elements must also become one dynamic unity. The apostle Paul writes in his

Second Letter to the Corinthians that we have the heavenly treasure in earthen vessels (4:7) and that the thorn in the flesh, which keeps a person grounded, is part of the heavenly revelation (12:17).

HEART CHAKRA: EXPERIENCING REDEMPTION

In many fairy tales, a hopeless situation suddenly takes a turn for the better. The prisoner is freed, people who have been turned to stone become alive again, or the despised are honored. Although this redemption generally occurs through the intervention of supernatural powers, the proper inner attitude of the fairy-tale hero or heroine contributes to the miracle of redemption becoming reality. For example, the prince in the tale called, "Bath Badgerd,"[15] hits the target with the last, decisive shot of the arrow because he closes his eyes when he shoots it. This means that he no longer trusts in his outer ability but turns his gaze inward. In the Russian version of "The Maiden without Hands,"[16] the girl receives new hands at the moment that she risks following a helper's instructions to use her nonexistent hands as if she had them.[17]

Sometimes the redemption occurs at the very last moment[18]—quite similar to the story that the New Testament tells of the criminal on the cross (Luke 23:42).

This redemption has no set pattern, since it happens in a way that corresponds to the individual fairy-tale heroine or hero. It also happens in such a way that it provides decisive help for the respective situation. It becomes clear that we each must take our own path leading to a goal that is right for us.

THROAT CHAKRA:
ENCOUNTER WITH THE SYMBOL

A symbol reveals an eternal meaning in an earthly manifestation. The variety of appearances in this world becomes transparent for the eternal world. And the interplay of the realities of this and the other world are the subject of fairy tales involving the secret of food. Examples of these are "The Wishing Table," "The Gold Ass," "Cudgel in the Sack," and the miracle pot in "Sweet Porridge," which produces abundant food at any time. In the tale of "The White Snake," tasting the snake gives a person the ability to understand the languages of the animals. On the other hand, the edible witch's cottage in "Hansel and Gretel" means a dangerous trap, just like eating the poisoned apple in "Snow White" and drinking the bewitched water in "Brother and Sister."

Fairy tales make it clear that food is not simply dead matter, but that it is connected to the spiritual world. Earthly food becomes a symbol for spiritual food—just like the Bible tells us of manna in the desert, the bread multiplied by Jesus, and the bread of the Last Supper, the Eucharist. All these are symbols for heavenly bread.

Our contemporary disregard for the correlation between the material and spiritual reality causes harm, not only at "The Last Supper,"[19] but also in fairy tales.[20]

THIRD EYE CHAKRA:
FOLLOWING THE INNER VOICE

What applies to the material realm also applies to the spiritual. The important thing is to differentiate between our own superficial desiring and the deeper desires of our true Self, which is our actual desire ("the will of God").

The inner voice, which means the voice of our true Self, is often expressed in fairy tales through the instructions of otherworldly helpers. The helpers know the alternatives and the solutions, even when the fairy-tale heroines and heroes are at the end of their wits. For example, the fox in "The Golden Bird" always has advice. The ant, duck, and bee in "The Queen Bee" and the toad in "The Three Feathers" help in solving difficult or unsolvable tasks. It's important for the fairy-tale heroine or hero to have a good relationship with animals. All fairy tales illustrating good relationships with animals lead to satisfactory solutions.[21] Over and over, the theme is paying attention to what is closest at hand, inconspicuous, and despised. Actual gold is to be found here, of all places. Like all the powers of the depths, the helpers may also have a dark aspect that should be recognized and banished.[22] This is why it is important to listen to both the voice of the depths as well as the voice of the rational mind.

CROWN CHAKRA: EVERYTHING IN ONE

In the crown chakra, the fairy-tale heroine and hero achieve a unity in which everything that life has to offer is contained and developed. In such a unity, all opposites are united—man and woman, old and young, the servant and the ruler.[23] As our brothers and sisters, the inner animals also belong to this unity.[24]

And God is above all things and in everything for in him we "live and move and have our being."[25] However, God is only rarely directly called by name in the fairy tales. The fairy tales speak of God like nature and history and our life speaks of God. It is a speaking without words. We encounter God in fairy tales whenever the sick are healed, the imprisoned are freed, the despised are elevated, and the arrogant are humbled. But we also encounter God when people who are meant for each other find each other despite all the obstacles, resistances, and intrigues, so that a new wholeness is created as a reflection of the union of Heaven and Earth, of human and God.[26]

The encounter with chakra symbolism in fairy tales can be an aid on the path to wholeness, and this means the path to God. Some fairy tales—the short ones, above all—have one single focal point that may become important and guiding in certain situations. In other fairy tales, the heroine or hero achieve partial goals.[27] Other fairy tales, especially the longer ones, describe the entire developmental process of the soul.[28] One example of this is "Mother Holle,"[29] which we will now explore in detail.

The Tale of Mother Holle in the Light of Chakra Symbolism

There was a widow who had two daughters, one who was beautiful and industrious, the other ugly and lazy. But Mother Holle was more fond of the ugly and lazy one because this was her own daughter. The pretty girl had to do all the housework and carry out the ashes, like a Cinderella. This poor maiden had to sit near a well by the road every day and spin and spin until her fingers bled. Now, one day it happened that the shuttle became quite bloody, and when the maiden leaned over the well to rinse it, the shuttle slipped out of her hand and fell to the bottom. She burst into tears, and ran to her stepmother to tell her about the accident. The stepmother gave her a terrible scolding and was very cruel. "If you let the shuttle fall in," she said, "you'd better get it out again."

The maiden went back to the well, but was so distraught that she jumped into the well to fetch the shuttle and there she lost consciousness. When she awakened and regained her senses, she found herself in a beautiful meadow, where the sun was shining and many thousands of flowers were growing. She walked across this meadow and came to a baker's oven full of bread. The bread was yelling at her, "Take me out! Take me out! Or else I shall burn. I've been baking long enough!" She went up to the oven and took out all the loaves, one at a time, with the baker's shovel.

Then she walked on until she came to a tree full of apples. "Shake me! Shake me!" the tree cried. "My apples are all ripe!" She shook the tree until the apples fell like raindrops, and she kept shaking until all the apples came down. After she gathered and stacked them in a pile, she walked on.

She finally came to a small cottage and saw an old woman looking out the window. This old woman had really big teeth, and the maiden was scared and wanted to run away. But the old woman cried after her, "Why are you afraid, my dear child? Stay with me. If you do all the housework properly, everything will turn out well for you. You must make my bed carefully and give it a good shaking until the feathers fly. Then it will snow on Earth, for I am Mother Holle." Since the old woman spoke so kindly, the maiden plucked up her courage and agreed to enter the old woman's home. She took care of everything to the old woman's satisfaction. She shook the bed so hard that the feathers flew about like snowflakes. And, in return, the old woman treated her well, never saying an unkind word and giving her roasted or boiled meat to eat every day.

After the maiden had spent some time with Mother Holle, she felt sad. She did not know what was bothering her, but finally realized she was homesick. Even though here was better than home, she still wanted to return to her family. At last she said to Mother Holle, "I've got a tremendous longing to return home, and while everything is wonderful here, I must return to my people."

"I'm pleased that you want to return home," Mother Holle responded, "and since you've served me so well, I, myself, shall bring you up there again."

She took the maiden by the hand and led her to a large door. When the door opened, and the maiden was standing right beneath the doorway, an enormous shower of gold came pouring down. All the gold stuck to the maiden so that she was completely covered with it! "I want you to have this because you've worked so hard," said Mother Holle, and she also gave her back the shuttle that had fallen into the well. Suddenly, the door slammed shut and the maiden found herself back up on Earth, not far from her step-mother's house. When she entered the yard, the cock was sitting on the well and crowed: "Cock-a-doodle-doo! My Golden Maiden, what's new with you?"

She went inside the house and found her stepmother, and since she was covered with so much gold, her step-mother and sister gave her a warm welcome.

She told them all about what happened, and when her stepmother heard how she had obtained so much wealth, she decided to arrange that her ugly and lazy daughter could have the same good fortune. She sent the ugly daughter to sit near the well and spin. But the ugly daughter made the shuttle bloody by sticking her fingers into a thornbush and pricking them. Then she threw the shuttle into the well and jumped in after it. Just like her sister, she reached the beau-tiful meadow and walked the same path. When she came to the oven, the bread cried out again, "Take me out! Take me out! Or else I shall burn! I've been baking long enough!"

But the lazy maiden answered, "I've no desire to get myself dirty!" She walked on, and came to the apple tree that cried out, "Shake me! Shake me! My apples are all ripe." However, the lazy maiden replied, "Are you serious? One of the apples could fall and hit me on my head." Thus she went on, until she came to Mother Holle's cottage. She was not afraid because she had already heard of the old woman's big teeth, and she hired herself out to her right away.

On the first day she made an effort to work hard and obey Mother Holle when the old woman told her what to do, for the thought of gold was on her mind. On the second day she started loafing, and on the third day she was even more lazy. She did not even want to get out of bed in the morning, nor did she make Mother Holle's bed as she should have. She certainly did not shake the bedding so the feathers flew. Soon Mother Holle became tired of this and dismissed the maiden from her service. The lazy maiden was quite happy to go and expected that now the shower of gold would come. Mother Holle led her to the door, but as the maiden was standing beneath the doorway, a big kettle of pitch came pouring down over her instead of gold.

"That's a reward for your services," Mother Holle said, and shut the door. The lazy maiden went home covered with pitch, and when the cock on the well saw her, it crowed: "Cock-a-doodle-doo! My Dirty Maiden, what's new with you?" The pitch did not come off the maiden and remained on her as long as she lived.

THE PATH OF THE GOLDEN MAIDEN

The path of the chakras begins with the root chakra, with being anchored in the world in which we live, in the world of consciousness, the here and now. It leads to the polarity chakra, which means entering the realm of the unconscious. As a result, the counterpole becomes visible. Then it continues on to the solar plexus chakra, where it becomes important to unify the poles revealed in the polarity chakra. This union then takes place in the heart chakra. (The solar plexus focuses on the process of unifying the opposites; this process has been concluded in the heart chakra. Wholeness is experienced.) In the throat chakra, we recognize the superficial world as a symbol of the enigmatic world. And the third eye involves the harmonization of our ego desires with the desires of our true Self. In the crown chakra, we finally experience the ultimate and deepest unity between Heaven and Earth, the completion of the path of individuation.

We can also discover these seven phases to a certain degree in the path of the Golden Maiden, whereby the symbolism of chakras two through five is also coupled with the four seasons. Let's look at the details of this process.

THE EXPERIENCE OF THE ROOT CHAKRA

A widow had two daughters—one beautiful and industrious, the other ugly and lazy. She was more fond of the ugly and lazy one because this was her own daughter. The pretty girl had to do all the housework and carry out the ashes like a Cinderella. This poor maiden had to sit near a well by the road every day and spin and spin until her fingers bled.

This section of the story contains the themes of the root chakra. It involves the conscious, superficial world, the world in which we live. This is not an idealized world in the fairy tale, but a very raw reality.

It is a world characterized by death, for the Golden Maiden's mother and father have died. The widow's first and second husbands have died, and the Dirty Maiden has lost her father. Since a father has died who had already lost his first wife and a widow's first and second husbands died, many people have been affected by death here.

The world of our fairy tale is also a world characterized by injustice. The Golden Maiden, who has lost her father and mother, and who is a diligent child, is treated badly, even cruelly, although she doesn't deserve this treatment, while her lazy half-sister is treated well without having earned it. The Golden Maiden is discriminated against as Cinderella was (and the listener is presumed to know the tale of Cinderella!). Cinderella is a figure who sits in the ashes and must do all the dirty work while being tormented by her sisters and stepmother.

In such situations in fairy tales, we can ask ourselves: are there also situations in my life in which I am discriminated against, in which others are preferred over me? Have I already experienced such situations? What kind of feelings do I or did I have? Perhaps I had the childhood experience of a competitive sports team being assembled and I was the last one chosen? People who experience this don't just experience it once, but repeatedly. How does it feel when things are like this? Or how is it when I am not chosen, or even rejected, when people select their partners for a dance or as part of a group process? Am I familiar with such injuries to my sense of self-worth? Or when I am passed over for promotions or jobs I apply for—how does it feel when other people are shown preference over me? It's good for us to imagine ourselves in these situations. There are few people who haven't experienced injuries and humiliations in at least one of these ways. However, when this becomes a constant experience, serious feelings of inferiority, or inferiority complexes, can develop!

In our fairy tale, we encounter the widow as a single parent. In this situation, there is a great danger of the bond between mother and daughter becoming too close. This may be a pulling together or a pushing away. The result is either a too negative, or a too positive, attachment of the daughter to the mother or the mother to the daughter. This develops into a mother complex.

In the story, the Golden Maiden develops a negative mother complex, and the Dirty Maiden develops a positive one.

The negative mother complex is characterized by the idea that we have to earn everything ourselves. We only receive recognition and love if we work for it. We must accomplish something, accomplish more, and accomplish even more in order to earn love and recognition for ourselves—and yet we still don't get it. Things do not work out because we must learn that we can't earn love. Love is a gift—we can't earn it. (This is the error of the frog in "The Frog King" when he thinks that he has a right to the girl's love because he has accomplished something. He also learns that we cannot earn love. He also has a negative mother complex. The fairy tale tells us that an "evil witch" has bewitched him.)[1]

The Dirty Maiden, the stepsister of the Golden Maiden, has a positive mother complex. This arises from the idea that the world is a big mother who permits everything. Everything falls in my lap; I don't have to make an effort to receive love and recognition. Everyone likes me. It may happen that this belief is confirmed, but these people must frequently also endure a bitter learning process.

The conspicuous characterization of the two girls involves the combination of "beautiful and industrious" and "ugly and lazy." In real life, things are often reversed: the less beautiful one must work more in order to earn recognition and assert herself, while the beautiful one has many things fall into her lap.

We must symbolically understand these fairy-tale relationships. "Beautiful" and "ugly" mean how an inner value is transmitted, meaning that a person who is "industrious" and who works on herself will gradually possess an inner beauty that ultimately penetrates to the outside world. On the other hand, someone who is "lazy" and who doesn't work on herself will gradually become gray and unsightly. The inner "ugliness" then inevitably becomes visible to the outside world as well.

The Golden Maiden must do all the work in the house, just like Cinderella. What does this mean? In the tale of Cinderella, we read:

> Cinderella's stepmother and stepsisters took her beautiful clothes, dressed her in an old gray smock, and gave her wooden shoes. "Look at the pretty princess and how well-dressed she is!" they exclaimed with laughter, leading her into the kitchen. They expected her to work there from morning till night. Cinderella had to get up before dawn, carry water to the house, start the fire, cook, and wash the clothes. In addition, her sisters did everything they could to cause her pain and make her look ridiculous. For instance, they dumped her peas and lentils into the hearth ashes so she had to sit there and pick them out. In the evening, when she was exhausted from working, she had no bed to go to, so she had to lie next to the hearth in the ashes.[2]

In the story about the Golden Maiden, spinning is mentioned in particular as her work. The girl sits near the well. (Since the fingers must be moistened when spinning, it is good to be close to water.) On a deeper level, "spinning" always also refers to spinning the thread of life. This also applies to the Cinderella phase of the Golden Maiden. Even in the terrible circumstances of life that we cannot avoid, the thread of life is still spun. These phases also belong to the pattern of our life.

The real world in which we live, which is characterized by the root chakra, is an essential aspect of our life. It is the foundation and ground for the roots in our life.

THE EXPERIENCE OF THE POLARITY CHAKRA AND SPRING

Now, one day we learn that the shuttle became quite bloody, and when the maiden leans over the well to rinse it, it slips out of her hand and falls to the bottom. The maiden bursts into tears, runs to her stepmother, and tells her about the accident. The stepmother gives her a terrible scolding and was very cruel. "If you've let the shuttle fall in," she says, "you'd better get it out again."

The maiden goes back to the well, but does not know where to begin. She is so distraught that she jumps into the well to fetch the shuttle, but she loses consciousness when doing so. She awakens and regains her senses and finds that she is in a beautiful meadow. The sun is shining and thousands of flowers are growing in this beautiful place.

The shuttle, as a symbol of the thread of life, now wants to go somewhere else. This is a situation of upheaval. The shuttle "slips" away, meaning that something is moving from within. This is similar to the ball in "The Frog King." It rolls away as if it had a life of its own. It symbolizes something that wants to move on. This rolling away is called the "mobile self," meaning the true Self[3] that has been set into motion. Something becomes independent—something unforeseen presses for further development. The girl first hurries to the mother figure. She stays in the old area because whatever is old and familiar—no matter how bad it is—is less threatening than something new and unknown. But the mother drives her back to the well. There is no more room for the girl in the old area.

Now the girl enters the world that is characterized by the polarity chakra. The leap into the well means a leap into the water. Going into the "water" means diving into the world of the unconscious. The unconscious is the womb of the Great Mother where negative mother experiences can be healed. The area of the unconscious is a counterworld to the world of consciousness. The girl is driven from within (by the shuttle that slips) and from the outside (by the mother who sends her back to the well, and is therefore also responsible for the descent into the unconscious) into the depths. This is a very important situation. Jesus characterizes this situation with the words: "If any [one] comes to me and hate not his father and mother . . . he cannot be my disciple" (Luke 14:26). This means: This is a radical letting go of what has existed up to now. Such a separation is necessary if we want to start on the inner journey.

The well is the place of transformation; it is the symbol of the mother's womb. Nicodemus in the New Testament is not so wrong in asking: "Can [a man] enter a second time into his mother's womb and be born?" (John 3:4). He naturally understands this in a superficial way as the return to the womb of his physical mother. But this actually involves returning to the primal mother, back to the world of the unconscious, into the womb of Mother Earth, the Great Mother, in order to begin life anew from that point.

By leaping into the well, the Golden Maiden experiences the counterworld: instead of the gray Cinderella-world of everyday life, the girl finds a sunny springtime meadow with thousands of flowers!

When a new beginning occurs in the life of any individual, the polarity is constellated in the unconscious. I once analyzed a severely depressed woman. During the course of the therapy, I suggested that she paint her inner situation. This was very difficult for her at first because she completely lacked any drive to do this, and the few pictures she made were very gray. Then one day she painted a picture with a gray and empty right half with a lovely blossoming flower in the left half. This was the beginning of an inner turn of the tide. Something had blossomed in her unconscious that was not yet visible to her conscious mind.

We occasionally encounter a similar blossoming of the unconscious in our dreams as well. Something can become visible in a dream that is not at all visible in the outside world, such as Jacob's dream in the Bible. The abandoned individual encounters angels and the heavens open (Genesis 28:10ff). People with a severely injured sense of self-worth sometimes have great difficulty accepting the positive inner counterworld that they encounter in dreams as reality, and therefore reject it: "But that's just a dream!" Yet, the dream world is just as real as the world of consciousness!

The "thousands of flowers" illustrate the colorfulness of the inner world and remind us of a statement by St. Paul, "For our light affliction, which is but for a moment, worketh for us a far more exceeding and eternal weight of glory" (II Corinthians 4:17). This does not mean we should wait until the other world, but also means the heaven within us. The "thousands of flowers" are compared to things that are so gray in everyday life.

The descent into the unconscious means the beginning of an inner journey. The girl "regains her senses." She had previously not lived within herself, but just beside herself.

The descent into the unconscious is a leap into the water. The green, juicy flowering meadow is also soaked with water. Water is the element associated with the polarity chakra.

The flowering meadow is the symbol of spring, and therefore of upheaval and a new beginning. In the meadow, the girl encounters the "green power" of Earth as the polarity to her gray everyday life. She experiences the light and warmth of the sun as a polarity to the cold mother. Vitality and warmth are Mother Holle's qualities, which the girl is now already encountering in the form of the flowering springtime meadow.

THE EXPERIENCE OF THE
SOLAR PLEXUS CHAKRA AND SUMMER

She walks across this meadow and soon comes to a baker's oven full of bread, but the bread is yelling, "Take me out! Take me out, or else I'll burn! I've been baking long enough!" She goes to the oven and takes out all the loaves one by one with the baker's shovel.

The baker's oven is a symbol for the solar plexus chakra. The element of this chakra is fire. In fire, the things that were previously separate are baked into one whole.

A communion text from the first century speaks of this: "Like this bread was scattered on the mountains and has been brought together to become one loaf of bread, your congregation shall be brought together from the ends of the earth into your kingdom."[4] This text comes from the experiences of an early Christian congregation in Syria. It was a custom that endured into the twentieth century. The

Christians there did not buy their communion bread from the baker but gathered the ears left lying in the harvested fields. They brought these in from the mountains and the hills so that all of the grain was together—grain next to grain. Then they had it ground and baked into one bread. The many scattered individual grains became one loaf. The transformation into one loaf of bread occurs through the heat of the fire. The hot fire also causes transformations in the baker's oven of our lives.

And how can we understand the individual grains in terms of our souls? They are the many split-off portions of the personality that want to be baked into one unity so that the wholeness of the individual, meaning the undivided personality, develops. This process of baking different elements into one is described in alchemy as a "cooking process" in a hermetically sealed vessel. This corresponds to the closed baker's oven in the heat of which the bread is baked. The hot baker's oven is an image of summer, which triggers the chemical processes in nature that allow the grain to become ripe.

The symbolism of the solar plexus chakra stands for the process that causes the unification of opposites, the process that aims for wholeness.

It is significant that the loaves of bread individually call out, "Take me out," and the girl takes them out one by one. The bread's cries mean that the right point in time has come. In the New Testament, this is expressed by the term *Kairos.*[5] This is the right point in time that should not be missed. It is important to listen to the voice of things; not just to the inner voice, but also to the voice of things that call us from the outside world. The baker's oven is also a symbol for the womb in which the child is carried. When the time is ripe, the child will enter into life.

For example, St. Augustine tells, in Book Eight, when he was feeling very depressed, that he heard a voice, a boy's or girl's voice, repeating over and over, "Take and read, take and read." He stopped crying and interpreted the incident as a divine command to open his book of Scripture and read the passage at which it should open. It was a book about St. Anthony, in which St. Anthony mentions reading from the gospel to the Romans when he felt he, himself, was being admonished. "Go, sell what thou hast . . . and follow Me." St. Anthony tells us that he was, upon reading that passage, and in that instant, converted to God. Augustine says that he was so moved reading this that all his own uncertainty vanished; he suddenly knew that he was called to serve God, and his life changed forever.[6] It is this call from the outside that happens to so many people who are making major changes in their lives. But we need to heed the call.

I also remember hearing about a man who quite coincidentally noticed a newspaper lying on a table in a restaurant. He had already walked by it. But the newspaper somehow called him back, and so he returned and leafed through it. He discovered an ad that had only been published in that newspaper. He responded to the ad, which then enriched his life in an extraordinary manner. The newspaper had called him from the outside. He heard this call and followed it.

Hearing the call involves taking advantage of opportunities and jumping at them when they arise, knowing that, "This is what's important right now!" Perhaps we then become afraid and say, "Not now—next time." But how do we know that there will be a next time? There usually isn't a next time. Right now a situation exists and asks you to participate. Although life will bring us other situations in the future if we do not take advantage of this one, they are not unlimited in number! Each situation is unique, and passes if we do not seize the opportunity. When life calls, this sometimes means, "Do what you are afraid of and fear will die a certain death!" This sentence has been a great help to me in some situations. Sometimes we need the "courage to make fools of ourselves." The call of life is more important than our image, or the reputation we have with others! There are things that want to be done right now.

Each loaf of bread calls, "Take me out," meaning that the individual tasks want to be taken seriously. We shouldn't neglect the details!

THE EXPERIENCE OF THE
HEART CHAKRA AND FALL

Our young maiden moves on and comes to a tree full of apples. "Shake me! Shake me!" the tree exclaims. "My apples are all ripe." She shakes the tree until the apples fall like raindrops, and she keeps shaking until they all come down. Then she gathers them and stacks them in a pile, and moves on again.

The apple is a symbol for wholeness. If we cut an apple crosswise, we find a mandala, the fivefold core in a circle, at its center. (See figure 32.)

Figure 32.   The apple mandala.

The apple symbolizes the heart chakra. The heart chakra is involved with wholeness and maturity. The process of the solar plexus chakra has come to its conclusion. Now it's important to bring in the harvest. While the loaves of bread individually call out, "Take me out!" although there are more of them, the tree says: "My apples are all ripe." The tree, which symbolizes wholeness, calls, "Shake me!" This means that the many apples are part of the whole; they are integrated into the unity. And once again, "things" are calling. And life calls with them. While the call is for "becoming" during summer, the call of fall is "being." This also applies to the seasons of life! After childhood, and the time of youth, comes the age of adulthood, and the time for maturity that no longer involves becoming—but being.

The heart chakra is the center of the chakras. The "lower" chakras have been traversed, and it is now time to rest before the "upper" chakras start.

An apple is not only the symbol for wholeness, it is also a symbol of Eros. Love is the connecting element that unifies us (the magnet is called *aimant* in French, meaning "the lover" that has an attracting and unifying effect). All of the opposites are united through love in the heart chakra. There is no becoming whole without Eros. Self-actualization is an erotic affair. It involves loving the inner figures so that they become closer to us.

THE EXPERIENCE OF THE THROAT CHAKRA AND WINTER

At last our young maident comes to a small cottage where an old woman is looking out the window. The old woman has big teeth and scares the maiden. She wants to run away, but the old woman cries after her, "Why are you afraid, my dear child? Stay with me, and if you do all the housework properly, everything will turn out well for you. Only you must make my bed nicely and carefully, and give it a good shaking so the feathers fly. Then it will snow on Earth, for I am Mother Holle." Since the old woman has spoken so kindly to her, the maiden plucks up her courage and agrees to enter her service. She takes care of everything to the old woman's satisfaction, and always shakes the bed so hard that the feathers fly about like snowflakes. In return, the old woman treats her well. She never says an unkind word to the maiden and gives her roasted or boiled meat every day.

Now Mother Holle (also called Mother Hulda) appears. Up to now, the experiences of the unconscious have been in the realm of the possible—the meadow, the baker's oven, the apple tree. They all exist in the superficial world, but now transcendence comes into play. This is the function of the throat chakra; earthly, superficial things become transparent for what is transcendent and deep. Another dimension has manifested.

Mother Holle introduces herself with the words, "I am Mother Holle." This is reminiscent of the epiphanies of the Greek deities, as we encounter them in Homer's hymns. This is how Demeter, for example, revealed herself as she appeared in a different form: "I am Demeter"[7] or Dionysius says, "I am Dionysius."[8] Jesus also used this "I am" formula in a number of places[9] (for example, when he encountered Saul, "I am Jesus"[10]). Through this formula, something of an enigmatic being is expressed.

Who is Mother Holle? Various pre-Christian goddess figures have flowed together in her, behind which is ultimately the *Magna Mater*, the Great Mother. Mother Holle is a holistic mother deity. Her name contains both *Hulda*, "graciousness," as well as *Hel* ("the underworld"). Hel is the underworld in the sense of the concealing element. This concealing of the Great Mother occurs in Hel (the cave). Both the giving mother and the taking mother live in the idea of Hel. The big teeth are an expression of the vitality we have already encountered in the springtime meadow, but also in gripping and biting and age. Mother Holle is an elementally powerful older deity. On the other hand, she is loving and calls the girl "dear child," and "never said an unkind word" to her. The Golden Maiden also encounters the counterworld to the outer world here.

After the experience of the rejecting mother in the superficial world, the Golden Maiden now encounters the accepting mother. Severe mother traumas can ultimately only be healed through the encounter with the Great Mother within the soul. No matter how many experiences a female may have with positive women, if she has had a deep-rooted negative mother experience, then these counter-experiences are not strong enough. Instead, the Great Mother must be constellated within her. Then the healing process begins because this holistic Great Mother also includes the negative mother experiences. The negative and positive mother are no longer experienced one after the other in the Great Mother but with each other. Everything is contained within the Great Mother. The encounter with the Great Mother is ultimately an encounter with God, since we find everything contained within God.

Tragically, there was a splitting off of the Great Mother—and therefore of Mother Holle—from the image of God in Christianity. Christianity has assigned the "positive" qualities of the Great Mother to the Virgin Mary and the "negative" ones to the witches. Through this split, the Virgin Mary has become excessively elevated and only "good," and consequently unearthly pale, and the witches are only "evil" and therefore too dark.

Polarizations are always "devilish." The *Dia-bolos* ("Devil") is the divider. On the other hand, we encounter God in the symbol, meaning the union of opposites. So this involves the poles finding their way back to each other. Thank God that Mother Holle's fairy tale has been preserved so that the Great Mother has remained alive among us at least in this one place!

Mother Holle's responsibility for the upper realms becomes apparent because of the snow. The fairy tale reveals the enigmatic Holle aspect because snow is the feather quilt that Mother Holle uses to cover Mother Earth, the Mother Earth that she is, herself. (The feathers also belong to Mother Holle, because geese are an attribute of the Great Mother.) When people see snow, they are reminded of Mother Holle. In some areas of Germany people still say when it snows, "Mother Holle is shaking her feather quilt." Like all natural processes, snowing also has a deeper dimension.

The housework that the girl does is also important. Before, it was the enslaving Cinderella work; but now it is liberating Mother Holle work. Keeping house for Mother Holle means practicing how to be a woman. Shaking the quilt makes this clear. Something occurs on a deeper level when we do something obvious on the superficial level.

THE EXPERIENCE OF THE THIRD EYE

After the maiden spends time with Mother Holle, she becomes very sad. At first she doesn't know what's bothering her, but finally realizes she is homesick. Even though everything is a thousand times better here than at home, she still has a desire to return. At last, she says to Mother Holle, "I've got a tremendous longing to return home, and even though everything is wonderful down here, I've got to return to my people."

"I'm pleased that you want to return home," Mother Holle responds, "and since you've served me so faithfully, I myself shall bring you up there again."

Everything comes to an end at some point, even the time of retreat. When we have set out on the inner journey "for a time," perhaps with the help of a self-realization course, or analysis, this period comes to an end at some point. It becomes clear within us that what we have experienced in our depths must also stand the test of everyday life. This "I've got to return" is reminiscent of the strong New Testament "must" in which doing something is unavoidable because of an inner feeling.[11] It is the longing for new activities that awakens within the Golden Maiden. After a phase of introversion, the extroversion comes again—a new countermovement. The experiences of the depths must prove themselves in everyday life. Spiritual experiences must be grounded, must be once again brought into everyday life. Mother Holle affirms this, since it is also her will. The Lord's Prayer Chakra Meditation associates this word with the third eye chakra: "Thy will be done on Earth as it is in Heaven."[12] This means that the will of the true Self has become the will of the ego. What "Mother Holle"—the Great Mother, the inner goddess—wants is also what the girl now wants. This harmony is the focus of the third eye.

THE EXPERIENCE OF THE CROWN CHAKRA

Mother Holle takes the maiden by the hand and leads her to a large door. When it opens and the maiden is standing right beneath the doorway, an enormous shower of gold comes pouring down, and all the gold sticks to her so she becomes completely covered with it. "I want you to have this because you've been so industrious," says Mother Holle, and she also gives her back the shuttle that had fallen into the well. Suddenly, the door closes and the maiden finds herself back up on Earth, not far from her stepmother's house. When she enters the yard, the cock is sitting on the well and crows, "Cock-a-doodle-doo! My Golden Maiden, what's new with you?"

She goes inside to her stepmother, and since she is covered with so much gold, her stepmother and stepsister give her a warm welcome.

The Golden Maiden is showered with gold, which means that she takes the gift from the depths into the upper world. The gold that falls on her head is symbolic of the crown chakra. Some fairy tales speak of a golden roof or golden hair, for example. Gold is a sign of something lasting, of perfection. Transformed, the Golden Maiden comes out of the depths. She is no longer a little girl, but "my golden maiden."

The shuttle surfaces again; the symbol of drudgery has not simply disappeared, it's still there because she brings it with her. Everything that we have experienced up to now is part of our life, but life goes on, and the thread of life continues to be spun. The Golden Maiden now has a new "aura," a new sense of self-worth. Even the stepmother and the stepsister are impressed by it and can't treat her like they did in the past. Now she has an inner strength. She is no longer the maladjusted, fearful girl who simply does what other people say. The Golden Maiden has a new awareness of her Self that makes other people somewhat timid around her.[13] When people have set off on an inner journey and

achieved a new aura, they are treated differently by their surrounding world—usually with more respect.

THE PATH OF THE DIRTY MAIDEN

Then the Golden Maiden tells them all about what happened to her, and when her stepmother hears how she obtained her wealth, the stepmother wants to arrange it so her
ugly and lazy daughter can have the same good fortune.
The ugly daughter now sits near the well, but she makes her
shuttle bloody by sticking her fingers into a thornbush and
pricking them. Then she throws the shuttle into the well
and jumps in after it. Just like her stepsister, she reaches the
beautiful meadow and walks along the same path. When
she comes to the oven, the bread cries out, "Take me out!"
But the lazy maiden answers, "I've no desire to get myself
dirty!" She moves on, and comes to the apple tree that cries
out, "Shake me! Shake me!" However, the lazy maiden
replies, "Are you serious? One of the apples could fall and
hit me on my head."

Thus the ugly daughter goes on, and when she comes
to Mother Holle's cottage, she is not afraid because she has
already heard of the old woman's big teeth, and she hires
herself out to her right away. On the first day she makes an
effort to work hard and obey Mother Holle when the old
woman tells her what to do, for the thought of gold is on
her mind. On the second day, she starts loafing, and on the
third day she loafs even more. Indeed, she doesn't want to
get out of bed in the morning, nor does she make Mother
Holle's bed as she should, and she certainly doesn't shake it
so hard the feathers fly. Soon Mother Holle becomes tired
of this and dismisses the maiden. The lazy maiden is quite

happy to go and expects the shower of gold. Mother Holle leads her to the door, but as the maiden is standing beneath the doorway, a big kettle of pitch comes pouring down over her instead of gold.

"That's a reward for your services," Mother Holle said, and shut the door. The lazy maiden goes home covered with pitch, and when the cock sees her, it crows: "Cock-a-doodle-doo! My Dirty Maiden, what's new with you?"

The pitch does not come off the maiden, and remains on her for as long as she lives.

The stepmother is envious of the Golden Maiden and wants to have the same good fortune for her own daughter. Envy can have its roots in a positive projection. Such projections can reveal our own possibilities to us.

However, the Dirty Maiden appears to be so indolent that she is too comfortable to even be envious. The mother is the one who takes action. When people are sent off on an inner journey by others, this is always a very questionable starting position! Quite frequently, the result is that imitation occurs instead of initiation, and copying instead of comprehension. Imitation is a path without transformation. For the Dirty Maiden, imitation is connected with a false concept of the goal, and the goal is only to achieve as great a gain as possible, as easily as possible.

The Dirty Maiden sets off on her inner journey without any pressure of suffering, and without any drive of her own, and with a false concept of the goal. This cannot end well. The Dirty Maiden does not act out of necessity, but throws herself into a spiritual adventure without any real reason to do so. A modern description of the Dirty Maiden says, "She does not notice the signs and calling of her unconscious. She runs away from herself. This is why she will be followed by bad luck (pitch) of her own unconscious throughout her entire life. She is a woman who can no longer find the strength to follow the call from the depths. She could be a consumer child, a television baby. She rushes through the stages of her life, completely isolated from everything that is beautiful. She may take drugs in order to experience herself, and so that she doesn't have to see the pitch that sticks to her."[14]

In such an "object-stage" interpretation of the fairy tale, the Dirty Maiden would be a completely different figure than the Golden Maiden. But in terms of the subjective stages, this applies: the Golden Maiden and the Dirty Maiden are two sides of the very same person.[15] These are two possibilities for how we shape our lives.

The actions taken by the Dirty Maiden are listless. She has absolutely no desire. The Dirty Maiden does not respond to the call of the things, she doesn't seize the Kairos, the right point in time to do what is necessary at the moment—and so she misses out on life. The Dirty Maiden is a "yes, but" person. "Yes, but" people always have a reason for not letting themselves get involved in the inner journey.

The Dirty Maiden is also not afraid of Mother Holle. Since she already knows everything theoretically—there is nothing more to surprise her. So she hears neither the "Don't be afraid" (she doesn't experience a *trememdum*[16]) nor the epiphany words, "I am Mother Holle" (she doesn't experience a *fascinosum*). The Dirty Maiden has no feeling for the time of departure. Mother Holle sends her away. The inner pitch, meaning the untransformed black depths, now also become visible externally. Those who do not set off on the inner journey will have the pitch stuck to them for an entire lifetime.

Two possibilities for these inner workings are shown to us in the figures of the Dirty Maiden and the Golden

Maiden. If we have lived the Dirty Maiden aspect up to now, we still have the possibility of starting anew at any time. In the process, it is naturally important that we first realize how we enact the pitch (bad luck) ourselves. It is an outer expression of our inner attitude. So it is important to change our inner attitude. Instead of imitating and constantly saying "yes, but," we must follow the call of life and then take the path that the Golden Maiden has shown us.

The Path of the Chakras
as the Path in Life

The path through the chakras is not only an individual path, it is also the path of humanity. C. G. Jung writes that even in history, we can observe the kundalini process. The first development was the belly consciousness of the primary human being who only noticed what was bothering him or what was in his stomach. The next development was the diaphragm consciousness of the Homeric person, who felt his emotions, which were expressed in tension states of breathing and changes in the heartbeat. Only the modern person has noticed that the head can also be affected. Before this time, it was not much more than a button on a feeling body."[1] This process of development can be recognized in a sculpture from the eleventh century[2] (see figure 33, page 178).

The circles on this sculpture can be interpreted as experiences of consciousness. They show that people in the Middle Ages experienced that something moved in their bodies, not only on the lower level (in the belly region) and not only in the middle (in the diaphragm and heart region), but also in the head. This means they felt the chakras in these areas.

In terms of modern human beings, C. G. Jung thought that the most highly developed peoples have reached Anahata,[3] while others still live in Svadhisthana or in Manipura.

Figure 33. Relief from Jacob's Church in Tuebingen: eleventh century.

It is said that what applies to humanity as a whole does not necessarily apply to individual human beings. I don't find this to be true. Each individual human being is called upon to take the path of the chakras time and again, and to intensify his or her experiences with the individual "stages." "Everything in the unconscious seeks outward manifestation, and the personality, too, desires to evolve out of its unconscious conditions and experience itself as a whole."[4]

The path of the chakras is the path we all take in life. This applies to both the entirety of our lives, as well as to the respective momentary situation of the chakra path in meditation. We can compare the path of the chakras with taking a trip.

The root chakra is the starting point for our travels. This is where we equip ourselves with the necessary clothing, provisions, and everything we will need for our trip. Earth offers us all of this.

In the polarity chakra, we risk departure. We are hit by an inner unrest and know that we must set off on the path, and we actually take the first steps on that path.

The solar plexus chakra represents the hardships of the path. We wander through deserts and wastelands, through glaring heat and fierce cold, threatened by all kinds of dangers.

The heart chakra symbolizes a rest stop. We rest and enjoy the calm. We eat and drink and enjoy community with other people. Then we set out on the path again.

In the throat chakra, we encounter traveling companions—angels and inner helpers. We encounter the other world and ourselves in them. These traveling companions keep us from false paths and protect us from danger.

The third eye represents our guide, the inner voice, and the voice of God that shows us the right path during our journey.

The crown chakra is the goal of our journey in life. It is the "Heavenly Jerusalem,"[5] toward which we all travel.

The path of the chakras is the symbol for our journey in life. In the chakra meditation, we can practice the individual stages of this path over and over—in retrospect and in looking forward—and mature. The process leads us toward self-actualization and wholeness as a result.

Notes

PART I: THE CHAKRAS—EAST AND WEST

The Path of Individuation and the Chakra Symbols

1. Arthur Avalon, *The Serpent Power* (Madras: Ganesh & Co., 1918).

2. See German language article by Linda Fierz and Toni Wolff, eds., *Bericht Ueber das Seminar von Prof. Dr. J. W. Hauer, 3–10 October, 1932*, published in mimeograph in Zurich, 1933; and C. G. Jung, *The Practice of Psychotherapy*, The Collected Works, vol. 16 (Princeton: Princeton University Press, 1954), §540ff. (The seminars edited by Linda Fierz and Toni Wolff are not available in English and have been translated from the German throughout this book; future references to this work will be abbreviated as Fierz-Wolff.)

3. Another book was published in English recently—actually it was released shortly after the German edition of my book was published. People reading my book may also want to explore the newest set of notes available. See C. G. Jung, *The Psychology of Kundalini Yoga: Notes of the Seminar Given in 1932*, Sonu Shamedasani, ed., Bollingen Series XCIX (Princeton: Princeton University Press, 1996).

4. C. G. Jung, *Psychological Types*, The Collected Works, vol. 6 (Princeton: Princeton University Press,

1971), §757. Future references to this volume will be to CW 6.

5. See M.-L. von Franz in C. G. Jung, *Man and His Symbols* (New York: Laurel/Dell, 1968), p. 163.

6. See von Franz in C. G. Jung, *Man and His Symbols*, p. 164.

7. See CW 6, §762.

8. See von Franz in C. G. Jung, *Man and His Symbols*, p. 163.

9. See C. G. Jung, *Man and His Symbols*, pp. 65–229; and CW 6, §756–762.

10. C. G. Jung, *The Archetypes and the Collective Unconscious*, The Collected Works, vol. 9i (Princeton: Princeton University Press, 1959), §81ff; C. G. Jung, *The Symbolic Life*, The Collected Works, vol. 18 (Princeton: Princeton University Press, 1976), §17; Linda Fierz and Toni Wolff, eds., *Bericht Ueber das Seminar von Prof. Dr. J. W. Hauer, 3–8 October, 1932*, pp. 153ff. (translated from the German). Future references to the Collected Works will be to CW 9i and CW 18.

11. C. G. Jung, *Man and His Symbols*, p. 224.

12. See Jung, CW9i, §81–82; Jung CW 18, §17; and Fierz-Wolff (in German), p. 153ff.

13. For example, a sculpture from the eleventh century in the Jakobuskirche (Jacob's Church) in Tuebingen, Germany, which is illustrated in this book on page 178).

14. See Jung, CW 18, §17.

15. See Paul Allen, ed., *A Christian Rosenkreutz Anthology* (Blauvelt, NY: Rudolf Steiner Publications, 1968). See section on the Chemical Wedding. There are other versions of this text available as well.

16. I have written on this subject as well. See A. Bittlinger, *Der Weg Jesu* (Münich: Droemer/Knaur, 1995), pp. 37ff, 147ff. See also the sections on the Bible and fairy tales in this book.

17. C. G. Jung, *The Visions Seminars,* Book One (Zurich: spring, 1976), p. 143.

18. C. G. Jung, *The Visions Seminars,* Book One, p. 143.

19. C. G. Jung, CW 18, §17.

20. C. G. Jung, CW 18, § 1331.

21. See C. G. Jung, CW 9i, figure 25, which is also reproduced in C. G. Jung and Richard Wilhelm, *The Secret of the Golden Flower* (London: Routledge & Kegan Paul, 1931), as Plate 5.

22. See CW 9i, §679.

23. C. G. Jung and Richard Wilhelm, *The Secret of the Golden Flower,* legend for figure 5.

24. See Jung, CW 9i, §679. Brackets mine.

25. C. G. Jung in Fierz-Wolff, p. 111. Translated from the German.

26. See J. W. Hauer in Fierz-Wolff, p. 60. Translated from the German.

27. See J. W. Hauer in Fierz-Wolff, p. 34.

28. See J. W. Hauer in Fierz-Wolff, p. 34ff.

29. See J. W. Hauer in Fierz-Wolff, p. 35.

The Chakra Symbols in Light of Analytical Psychology

1. C. G. Jung in Linda Fierz and Toni Wolff, eds., Bericht *Usher das Seminar von Prof. Dr. J. W. Hauer, 3–8 October, 1933* (Zurich: Mimeograph from the Psychologischen Club, Zurich, 1933). This and other passages from this seminar are translated from the German; and referenced as Fierz-Wolff.

2. C. G. Jung in Fierz-Wolff, p. 112.

3. C. G. Jung in Fierz-Wolff, p. 112.

4. C. G. Jung in Fierz-Wolff, p. 131.

5. C. G. Jung in Fierz-Wolff, p. 121.

6. C. G. Jung, *The Visions Seminars,* Books One and Two (Zurich: spring, 1976), Book Two, p. 420.

7. C. G. Jung, *The Visions Seminars,* Book Two, p. 421.

8. C. G. Jung, *The Visions Seminars,* Book Two, pp. 406 ff.

9. C. G. Jung, *The Visions Seminars,* Book One, p. 143.

10. Marie-Louise von Franz, *Alchemy: An Introduction to the Symbolism and Psychology* (Toronto: Inner City, 1980), p. 222.

11. C. G. Jung, *The Visions Seminars,* Book Two, pp. 407–408.

12. C. G. Jung, "Psychological Commentary on Kundalini Yoga, Lecture Three, 26 October, 1930," in *Spring,* 1976.

13. C. G. Jung in Fierz-Wolff, p. 134. The elephant is the symbolic animal of the Vishudhi.

14. C. G. Jung, "Psychological Commentary on Kundalini Yoga, Lecture Three," p. 6.

15. C. G. Jung, "Psychological Commentary on Kundalini Yoga, Lecture Three," pp. 8–9.

16. C. G. Jung, "Psychological Commentary on Kundalini Yoga, Lecture Three," p. 9.

17. C. G. Jung, "Psychological Commentary on Kundalini Yoga, Lecture, Three," p. 17.

18. Jung calls this inner seeing the "eyes of the background." See *Memories, Dreams, Reflections* (New York: Pantheon, 1963), p. 50.

19. See A. Bittlinger, *Das Vaterunser* (Munich: Kosel Verlag, 1990), pp. 87ff.

20. C. G. Jung, "Psychological Commentary on Kundalini Yoga, Lecture Three," p. 17.

21. C. G. Jung, "Psychological Commentary on Kundalini Yoga, Lecture Three," p. 19.

22. C. G. Jung, "Psychological Commentary on Kundalini Yoga, Lecture Three," p. 17.

23. C. G. Jung in Fierz-Wolff, p. 144.

24. C. G. Jung, "Psychological Commentary on Kundalini Yoga, Lecture Three," p. 18.

25. M.-L. von Franz, *Alchemy,* p. 223.

PART II: THE CHAKRAS—DEFINITIONS

The Chakra Symbols and the Path of the Chakras

1. See S. Wallimann, *Umpolung* (Freiburg: Bauer Verlag, 1988), pp. 4ff; as well as C. G. Jung, *The Symbolic Life*, The Collected Works, vol. 18 (Princeton: Princeton University Press, 1976), §1331; A. Bittlinger, *Das Vaterunser* (Munich: Kosel Verlag, 1990), pp. 12ff.

The Root Chakra

1. C. G. Jung in Linda Fierz and Toni Wolff, eds., *Bericht Ueber das Seminar von Prof. Dr. J. W. Hauer, 3–8 October, 1932* (Zurich: Mimeograph from Psychologischen Club, Zurich, 1933), pp. 110ff.

2. C. G. Jung in Fierz-Wolff, p. 131.

3. M. L. von Franz, in C. G. Jung, *Man and His Symbols* (New York: Laurel/Dell, 1968), p. 161.

4. See S. Freud, *The Basic Writings of Sigmund Freud*, E. A. Brill, ed. (New York: Modern Library/Random House, 1938), pp. 69–86.

5. C. G. Jung, *Psychological Types*, The Collected Works, vol. 6 (Princeton: Princeton University Press, 1971). Future references to this title will be to CW 6.

6. See A. Bittlinger, *Heimweh nach der Ewigkeit* (Munich: Kosel Verlag, 1993), pp. 74ff.

7. There are tests we can take to determine our individual type. But I think it is better to gradually become

familiar with our strengths and weaknesses through our everyday interactions with other people and with the accompanying text. You may also want to explore C. G. Jung's *Psychological Types* (CW 6).

8. See A. Bittlinger, *Das Geheimnis der Christlichen Feste: Tiefenpsychologische und Astrologische Zugaenge* (Munich: Kosel Verlag, 1995), pp. 218–223.

9. See A. Bittlinger, *Christlicher Glaube und Astrologie* (Kindhausen: Metanoia, 1996).

10. See C. G. Jung, CW 6, §801.

11. See C. G. Jung, CW 6, §798.

12. See C. G. Jung, CW 6, §799.

13. See C. G. Jung, *Alchemical Studies*, The Collected Works, vol. 13 (Princeton: Princeton University Press, 1967), figure 26. Future references will be to CW 13.

14. See C. G. Jung, CW 13, §334.

The Polarity Chakra

1. References to the Bible are to the King James Version.

2. C. G. Jung, *Psychological Types*, The Collected Works, vol. 6 (Princeton: Princeton University Press, 1971), §804.

3. C. G. Jung in Linda Fierz and Toni Wolff, eds., *Bericht Ueber das Seminar von Prof. Dr. J. W. Hauer, 3–8 October, 1932* (Zurich: Mimeograph Psychologischen

Club, Zurich, 1933), p. 131. Translated from the German; future references will be to Fierz-Wolff.

4. C. G. Jung in Fierz-Wolff, p. 131.

5. According to C. G. Jung, "Psychological Commentary on Kundalini Yoga, Lecture One, 12 October, 1932," in *Spring,* 1975, p. 14. Jung also compares the kundalini with the lady for whom the medieval knight undertakes the greatest exertions. The "divine impulse" corresponds with the "divine must" in the New Testament; for example, see John 4:4.

6. J. W. Hauer in Fierz-Wolff, p. 58.

7. C. G. Jung, "Psychological Commentary on Kundalini Yoga, Lecture One," p. 11.

8. C. G. Jung in Fierz-Wolff, p. 12.

9. "The acquaintance with the Leviathan means either rebirth or destruction," C. G, Jung in "Psychological Commentary . . . ," p. 11; also think of the story of Jonah in the Old Testament.

10. C. G. Jung, "Psychological Commentary . . . ," p. 11.

11. On the topic of projection, see M.-L. von Franz, *Projection and Re-Collection in Jungian Psychology* (La Salle, IL: Open Court, 1980), and P. Schellenbaum, *Wir Sehen uns im Andern* (Kindhausen: Metanoia, 1986).

12. I quote from J. Firges, *Der Blick bei Jean-Paul Sartre* (Kindhausen: Metanoia, 1996), 27f. Translated from German.

13. See Morton Kelsey, *Caring* (New York: Paulist Press, 1981).

14. Her case was published in A. *Bittlinger, Das Vaterunser* (Munich: Kosel Verlag, 1990), p. 38.

The Solar Plexus Chakra

1. C. G. Jung in Linda Fierz and Toni Wolff, eds., *Bericht Ueber das Seminar von Prof. Dr. J. W. Hauer, 3–8 October, 1932* (Zurich: Mimeograph Psychologischen Club, Zurich, 1933), p. 121. Future references will be to Fierz-Wolff.

2. C. G. Jung in Fierz-Wolff, p. 126. Translated from the German.

3. Swami Amaldas, *Jesu Abba Consciousness* (Bangalore: Asian Trading Corp., 1986), p. 107.

4. C. G. Jung, *The Visions Seminars,* Book Two (Zurich: Spring, 1976), p. 421.

5. This woman's case is mentioned in my book, *Das Vaterunser* (Munich: Kosel Verlag, 1990), p. 54.

6. See A. Bittlinger, *Der Weg Jesu* (Munich: Droemer/ Knauer, 1995), pp. 131ff.

7. C. G. Jung, *Alchemical Studies,* The Collected Works, vol. 13 (Princeton: Princeton University Press, 1967), figure 26. The patient's first picture is reproduced here as figure 11 on page 39. Future references will be to CW 13.

8. C. G. Jung, CW 13, figure 28. The patient is discussed in Jung's text.

9. C. G. Jung, CW 13, §337.

10. On the other hand, she still finds herself in the polarity chakra with her flipperlike feet.

11. M.-L. von Franz, *Projection and Re-Collection in Jungian Psychology* (La Salle, IL: Open Court, 1980), pp. 9–19; also see Luke 5:7.

12. See II Corinthians 12:7ff.

13. See A. Bittlinger, *Heimweh Nach der Ewigkeit* (Munich: Kosel Verlag, 1993), pp. 80f.

14. See M.-L. von Franz in C. G. Jung, *Man and His Symbols* (New York: Laurel/Dell, 1968), pp. 186, 198.

15. See M.-L. von Franz in C. G. Jung, *Man and His Symbols*, p. 195.

16. See M.-L. von Franz in *Man and His Symbols*, p. 206.

The Heart Chakra

1. Swami Almadas, *Jesu Abba Consciousness* (Bangalore: Asian Trading Corp., 1986), p. 107.

2. See *The Gospel According to Thomas* (New York: Harper & Brothers, 1959), p. 29:50.

3. See A. Bittlinger, *Im Kraftfeld des Heiligen Geistes* (Marburg: Oakumenischer Verlag, 1968), p. 124.

4. This and the quoted material above is from C. G. Jung in Fierz-Wolff, p. 123. Translated from the German.

5. C. G. Jung, *The Visions Seminars,* Book Two (Zurich: Spring, 1976) pp. 406ff.

6. See A. Bittlinger, *Das Vaterunser* (Munich: Kosel Verlag, 1990), pp. 73ff.

7. See C. G. Jung, *The Visions Seminars,* Book Two, p. 406.

8. A. Bittlinger, *Es War Einmal* (Munich: Droemer/Knauer, 1994), pp. 227, 371n.

9. See D. H. Salman, "La Regression au Service du Moi dans l'Experience religieuse," in *Archiv fuer Religionspsychologie,* vol. 9 (Paris, 1967), pp. 49ff.

10. C. G. Jung, *The Visions Seminars,* Book Two, p. 421.

11. See A. Bittlinger, *Es War Einmal,* p. 223.

The Throat Chakra

1. C. G. Jung, "Psychological Commentary on Kundalini Yoga, Lecture Three, 26 October, 1932," in *Spring,* 1976, p. 1.

2. A. Rosenberg, *Engel und Daemon* (Munich: Prestel Verlag, 1967), pp. 58ff.

3. See J. W. Hauer in Linda Fierz and Toni Wolff, eds., *Bericht Ueber das Seminar von Prof. Dr. J. W. Hauer, 3–8 October, 1932* (Zurich: Mimeograph Psychologischen Club, 1933), p. 72; Hebrew *rakia* (Genesis 1:6-8; see the blue color of the sky!).

4. See J. W. Hauer in Fierz-Wolff, p. 72; *sthula* is the material aspect that can be perceived with the senses; see also Fierz-Wolff, p. 18.

5. C. G. Jung in Fierz-Wolff, p. 133. Translated from the German.

6. C. G. Jung in Fierz-Wolff, p. 134. Translated from the German.

7. Plato, *Apology*. See any of the major translations. For example, *The Dialogues of Plato*, Benjamin Jowett, trans. (Chicago: Encyclopaedia Britannica, 1952), p. 31.

8. Acts of the Apostles 16:7.

9. C. G. Jung, "Psychological Commentary . . . ," p. 6.

10. See C. G. Jung, "Psychological Commentary . . . ," pp. 9ff.

11. C. G. Jung, "Psychological Commentary . . . ," p. 5.

12. C. G. Jung, *Psychological Types*, The Collected Works, vol. 6 (Princeton: Princeton University Press, 1971), §790, 816–824.

13. C. G. Jung, *Aion*, The Collected Works, vol. 9i (Princeton: Princeton University Press, 1976), §80.

The Third Eye Chakra

1. C. .G. Jung, "Psychological Commentary on Kundalini Yoga, Lecture Three, 26 October, 1932," in *Spring*, 1976, pp. 16–17.

2. C. G. Jung, "Psychological Commentary . . . ," p. 17.

3. John 1:18; Colossians 1:15.

4. Romans 8:29; our Self (meaning who we actually are) is a reflection of Christ.

5. C. G. Jung in Linda Fierz and Toni Wolff, eds., *Bericht Ueber das Seminar von Prof. Dr. J. W. Hauer, 3–8 October, 1932* (Zurich: Mimeograph Psychologischen Club, Zurich, 1933), p. 134.

6. See A. Bittlinger, *Das Vaterunser* (Munich: Kosel Verlag, 1990), pp. 87 ff.

7. C. G. Jung, "Psychological Commentary . . . ," p. 17.

The Crown Chakra

1. C. G. Jung in Linda Fierz and Toni Wolff, eds., *Bericht Ueber das Seminar von Prof. Dr. J. W. Hauer, 3–8 October, 1932* (Zurich: Mimeograph Psychologischen Club, Zurich, 1933), p. 87. Translated from the German; future references will be to Fierz-Wolff.

2. C.G. Jung, "Psychological Commentary on Kundalini: Yoga, Lecture Three 26 October, 1932," in *Spring,* 1976, p. 17.

3. See Revelation 21:2.

4. C. G. Jung in Fierz-Wolff, p. 70. Translated from the German.

5. According to the teachings of the Cabala, Jod is also contained in the first letter of the Bible, namely reversed at the right bottom in Beth (ß). Since Hebrew is

written from the right to the left, the Holy Scripture actually begins with this "Jod."

6. Instead of this, the Jews say, "Adonai," "Heaven," or "Name."

7. This differentiation leads to polarization (Genesis 3:12), which was only overcome through the spirit of Christ (Galatians 3:28, "there is neither Jew nor Greek, there is neither bond or free, there is neither male nor female . . ."), and thereby transformed into a dynamic polarity.

8. In the Bible, paradise (Genesis 2) is the symbol for undeveloped unity. On the other hand, the heavenly Jerusalem (Revelation 21ff.) is symbolic of the developed, or differentiated, unity.

9. John 7:38 describes the reality that the downward-oriented lotus blossom symbolizes. In the New Testament, not only the reality that can be experienced immediately is described, but also a preview up to the end of the great World Year (See A. Bittlinger, *Die Weltszeitalter*, Kindhausen: Metanoia, 1997) and even beyond this time. So what Jesus said will never be outdated. The opposite is true: we are only gradually approaching an understanding of what Jesus said. Accordingly, it says in the Gospel of John: "I have yet many things to say to you, but you cannot bear them now" (John: 16:12). Much of what Jesus said is still "unbearable" and "incomprehensible."

10. Arthur Avalon, *The Serpent Power* (Madras: Ganesh & Co., 1918).

11. Revelation 4:9–11.

12. C. Leadbeater, *The Chakras* (Wheaton: Quest/ Theosophical, 1973), p. 10.

PART III: THE CHAKRAS AND COLOR

The Symbolic Colors of the Chakras

1. There are impressive illustrations of these "natural" colors in Leadbeater's book, *The Chakras* (Wheaton: Quest/Theosophical, 1973).

2. There are more modern books on the chakras that show the colors. One such example would be the recently published Ashok Bedi, *Path to the Soul*. Bedi has written about the psychological meaning of the chakras and provided lovely modern illustrations of them (Weiser 2000). A discussion of the Indian meanings of the chakras is also in Jung's lectures, edited by Fierz-Wolff and referenced here. And perhaps readers will also want to explore Jung's *The Psychology of Kundalini Yoga* recently published by Princeton University Press.

3. J. W. Hauer differentiates between collective symbols, group symbols, and individual symbols; see Linda Fierz and Toni Wolff, eds., *Bericht Ueber das Seminar Prof. Dr. J. W. Hauer, 3–8 October, 1932* (Zurich: Mimeograph Psychologischen Club, Zurich, 1933), pp. 88ff. The personal chakra colors are "individual" symbols.

Orange—the Polarity Chakra

1. See A. Bittlinger, *Das Geheimnis der Christlichen Feste* (Munich: Kosel Verlag, 1995), pp. 246ff.

Yellow—the Solar Plexus Chakra

1. Ezekial 1:12ff.

Green—the Heart Chakra

1. Book of Sirach 40: 22 in *The Apocrypha of the Old Testament* (New York: Thomas Nelson, 1957).

2. Do you remember the Grimm's fairy tale that speaks of two brothers who turned green with envy? Shakespeare also mentions green with jealousy in *Othello* and *The Merchant of Venice*.

3. From Jean Chevalier and Alain Gheerbrandt, *Dictionnaire des Symboles* (Paris, 1982), p. 1003.

4. Readers may want to explore the world of the dervish, the mystical side of Sufism.

5. Greek Christians also discovered evidence of the Christ monogram in the word *chloros* (green) because the first syllable of *chloros* begins with an *x* (chi = ch) and the second syllable with an *r* (ro = r) (✣) These are the beginning letters of *Christus*.

Blue—the Throat Chakra

1. See A. Bittlinger, *Das Vaterunser* (Munich: Kosel Verlag, 1990), pp. 81ff.

Violet—the Third Eye Chakra

1. Genesis 1:2.

2. Ingrid Riedel, *Farben* (Stuttgart: Kreuz Verlag, 1983), p. 138.

PART IV: THE CHAKRAS AND INNER ANIMALS

The Personal Chakra Animals

1. Ezekial 1:10; Revelation 4:7.

2. E. S. Galegos, *The Personal Totem Pole* (Santa Fe: Bear & Co., 1987).

3. See A. Bittlinger, *Christlicher Glaube und Astrologie* (Kindhausen: Metanoia, 1996). This idea is more easily understood when you consider the natural houses of the zodiac, with Aries on the 1st house cusp. When a timed chart is calculated, Aries will not necessarily be on the cusp of the 1st house, and any one of the other eleven signs could be present there. The planets in the "natural" horoscope are also different than they are in the timed horoscope: for example, while the Sun rules Leo and the 5th house, it may not be there in your chart; while Venus rules Taurus and Libra, your Venus may be placed in another sign, and may not be located in the 2nd house of Taurus, or the 7th house of Libra.

4. Quoted in *Esotera* 2/97, p. 30.

5. Oral report from Christian Lerch, who did this imaginary journey with his class in school.

6. C. G. Jung, *Civilization in Transition*, The Collected Works, vol. 10 (Princeton: Princeton University Press, 1964), §32.

PART V: THE CHAKRAS IN WESTERN INTERPRETATION

The Path of the Chakras in the Bible

1. I Peter 2:21.

2. See C. G. Jung, *Psychology and Religion: West and East*, The Collected Works, vol. 16 (Princeton: Princeton University Press, 1964/1970), §146.

3. See Matthew 15:19; also the voice of Satan in Matthew 4:1ff, and Luke 4:1ff.

4. See Matthew 12:34; Luke 6:45.

5. Matthew 4:1ff; Mark 1:12ff; Luke 4:1ff; also see Matthew 16:22ff.

6. See the parables of Jesus, such as Matthew 13, Luke 15, and John 15:1–8.

7. For example, Christ's feeding of the multitudes and the interpretation in John 6:1–15 and John 6:22ff, or the raising of the dead in John 11:1ff, and the interpretation in John 11:35ff.

8. See A. Bittlinger, *Der Weg Jesu* (Munich: Droemer/ Knauer, 1995), pp. 37ff.

9. See Mark 1:12ff.

10. See Luke 23:12; Ephesians 2:14, and so forth.

11. See A. Bittlinger, *Im Kraftfeld des Heiligen Geistes* (Marburg: Oakumenischer Verlag, 1968), p. 124.

The Lord's Prayer as a Chakra Meditation

1. See Luke 5, 8:7, 6ff, and so forth.

2. See Matthew 26:41, 69ff.

3. See Matthew 18:21ff.

4. Luke 22:35.

5. Matthew 14:13ff; Matthew 6:30ff; Luke 9:10ff; John 6:5ff.

6. John 6:26–35.

7. The Greek word *epi-ousios* means both "daily" bread (the bread that nourishes the body), and "essential" bread (the bread that nourishes the soul).

8. This corresponds with the "return" from the crown chakra to the root chakra. With regard to this, J. W. Hauer writes in Linda Fierz and Toni Wolff, eds., *Bericht Ueber das Seminar von Prof. Dr. J. W. Hauer, 3–8 October 1932* (Zurich: Mimeograph Psychologischen Club, Zurich, 1933), p. 87, that the kundalini returns to Muladhara through all the chakras and gives these chakras, meaning all these different areas, a new power, as well as a new perspective for the human being. And now the yogi actually lives in the worldly, earthly life in a new way from this moment on. This could also be said of a person who has experienced the Lord's Prayer in his or her life and then returns to the AMEN of the Lord's Prayer.

9. See Revelation 21:2.

Chakra Symbolism in Fairy Tales

1. See the tale of "Faithful John," *The Complete Grimm's Fairy Tales* (New York: Pantheon/Random House, 1944).

2. For example, Blue Beard.

3. See "The White Bride and the Black Bride," in *The Complete Grimm's Fairy Tales*.

4. The Virgin Mary's child in "Our Lady's Child," in *The Complete Grimm's Fairy Tales*.

5. See "The Grave-Mound."

6. In "Faithful John" they say there are one hundred rooms! We also encounter the motif of the unknown rooms in many dreams.

7. "Mother Holle," in *The Complete Grimm's Fairy Tales*.

8. "Cinderella," and other stories.

9. "The Three Feathers," and other stories.

10. "The Two Travelers," "The Two Brothers," and "The Goose Girl."

11. See A. Bittlinger, *Das Vaserunser* (Munich: Kosel Verlag, 1990), p. 47.

12. See "The Golden Bird," "The Wishing Table," "The Gold-Ass," and "The Cudgel in the Sack," or "The Water of Life."

13. See "The Fisherman and His Wife."

14. "The Golden Bird."

15. See M.-L. von Franz, *Individuation in Fairy Tales* (Zurich: spring, 1975), pp. 60–67.

16. *Reussische Volksmaerchen* (Düsseldorf/Köln: Eugen Diederichs Verlag, 1959), p. 137.

17. One symbol for such "trust" is also the bumblebee. I read that the average bumblebee weighs a little more than 4 grams, has a wing surface of 1.45 cm² with a surface angle of 6 degrees. According to the law of aerodynamics, the bumblebee cannot fly. But the bumblebee doesn't know this.

18. For example, see "Our Lady's Child."

19. II Corinthians 11:28ff.

20. For example, see "Sweet Porridge," and other fairy tales.

21. "The Christian love of your neighbor can extend to the animal, too, the *animal in us*," C. G. Jung, *Civilization in Transition*, The Collected Works, vol. 10 (Princeton: Princeton University Press, 1964/1970), §32.

22. See "The Spirit in the Bottle," and "Rumpelstiltskin."

23. This becomes especially clear in "Faithful John." Also see Galatians 3:28: "There is neither Jew nor Greek, there is neither bond nor free, there is neither male nor female; for you are all one in Christ Jesus."

24. See conclusion of "The Golden Bird."

25. Acts of the Apostles 17:28.

26. Revelation 22:2 and 9.

27. See "The Nail," or "Hansel and Gretel" and "Little Red-Cap."

28. See "The Goose Girl," "The Golden Bird," or "Faithful John."

29. There are many versions of "Mother Holle." This is my version.

The Tale of Mother Holle

1. See A. Bittlinger, *Es War Einmal* (Munich: Droemer/Knauer, 1994), pp. 112ff, 124. Readers who read German can look at this title for many references to what we discuss here in this chapter.

2. One version of "Cinderella," the Grimm's fairy tale.

3. In analytical psychology, the Self (or the "true Self") means the overall personality, which includes both the conscious and the unconscious area of the human psyche. The Self "expresses the unity of the overall personality as a whole." C. G. Jung, *Psychological Types*, The Collected Works, vol. 6 (Princeton: Princeton University Press, 1971), §789.

4. See A. Bittlinger, *Das Abendmahl* (Craheim: Rolf Kuhne Verlag, 1969), pp. 33ff.

5. See A. Bittlinger, *Die Weltzeitalter* (Kindhausen: Metanoia, 1997), pp. 27ff.

6. See Saint Augustine, *The Confessions*, in *Great Books of the Western World* (Chicago: Encyclopaedia Britannica, 1952), VIII, p. 61.

7. *Homeric Hymns*, II, 268.

8. *Homeric Hymns*, VIII, 56.

9. See John 8:12, 10:11, 11:25, and so forth.

10. Acts of the Apostles 9:5.

11. See A. Bittlinger, *Der Weg Jesu* (Munich: Droemer/ Knauer, 1995), pp. 30ff.

12. See A. Bittlinger, *Das Vaterunser* (Munich: Kosel Verlag, 1990), pp. 87ff.

13. See Acts of the Apostles 5:13.

14. S. Ruettner Cova, *Frau Holle* (Basel: Sphinx Verlag, 1986), p. 66.

15. In the German television film, "Frau Holle" (made in Germany in 1961 with Lucie Englisch and Madeleine Binsfeld), a prince wants to take the Golden Maiden back to his castle after she has returned from Mother Holle. The Golden Maiden is only willing to go if she can also take the Dirty Maiden and the stepmother with her, so both of them ride along on the backseat of the coach. This is a beautiful image because there is no wholeness without integration of the opposites.

16. See A. Bittlinger, *Religion und Kulthandlungen im Lichte der Analytischen Psychologie* (Kindhausen: Metanoia, 1995), pp. 8ff.

The Path of the Chakras as the Path in Life

1. C. G. Jung in Linda Fierz and Toni Wolff, eds., *Bericht Ueber das Seminar von Prof. Dr. J. W. Hauer, 3–8 October, 1932* (Zurich: Mimeograph Psychologischen Club, Zurich, 1933), p. 102. In this context, Jung points out

African cliff pictures that depict people with extraordinarily long bodies . . . upon which some have very small or vaguely outlined human or animal heads. (Future references to this publication will be to Fierz-Wolff.)

2. Sculpture in St. Jacob's Church in Tuebingen, Germany, eleventh century.

3. C. G. Jung in Fierz-Wolff, pp. 134ff.

4. C. G. Jung, *Memories, Dreams, Reflections* (New York: Pantheon, 1961), p. 3.

5. Revelation 21ff.

Bibliography

Allen, Paul, ed. *A Christian Rosenkreutz Anthology*. "The Chemical Wedding of Christian Rosenkreutz." Blauvelt, NY: Rudolf Steiner Publications, 1968.

Amaldas, Swami. *Jeshu Abba Consciousness*. Bangalore: Asian Trading Corp., 1986.

Andrae, V.: *Chymische Hochzeit*. Stuttgart: Calwer, 1976.

The Apocrypha of the Old Testament. New York: Thomas Nelson and Sons, 1957.

Augustine. *The Confessions*. In *Great Books of the Western World*, vol. 18. Morton Adler, ed. Chicago: Encyclopaedia Brittannica, 1952.

Avalon, Arthur (Sir John Woodroffe). *The Serpent Power*. Madras: Ganesh & Co., 1918.

Bittlinger, Arnold. *Das Abendmahl*. Craheim: Rolf Kühne Verlag, 1969.

———. *Christlicher Glaube und Astrologie*. Kindhausen: Metanoia, 1996.

———. *Es war einmal: Grimms Maerchen im Lichte von Tiefenpychologie und Bibel*. Munich: Dromer/Knauer Verlag, 1994.

———. *Das Geheimnis der christlichen Feste: Tiefenpsychologische und Astrologische Zugaenge*. Munich: Kosel Verlag, 1995.

————. *Heimweh nach der Ewigkeit*. Munich: Kosel Verlag, 1993.

————. *Im Kraftfeld des Heiligen Geistes*. Marburg: Oaku-menischer Verlag, 1968.

————. *Religion und Kulthandlungen im Lichte der Analytis-chen Psychologie*. Kindhausen: Metanoia, 1995.

————. *Das Vaterunser: erlebt im Licht von Tiefenpsychologie un Chakrenmeditation*. Munich: Kosel Verlag, 1990.

————. *Der Weg Jesu: Urbild Unseres Weges*. Munich: Dromer/Knauer Verlag, 1995.

————. *Die Weltzeitalter*. Kindhausen: Metanoia, 1997.

Chevalier, Jean and Alain Gheerbrandt. *Dictionaire des Symbols*. Paris, 1982.

The Complete Grimm's Fairy Tales. New York: Pantheon, 1944.

Cova, S. Ruettner. *Frau Holle*. Basel: Sphinx Verlag, 1986.

Fierze, Linda and Toni Wolff, eds. *Bericht ueber das Seminar von Prof. Dr. J. W. Hauer, 3–8 October, 1932*. Zurich: Psychologischen Club, Zurich, Mimeograph, 1933.

Firges, J. *Der Blick bei Jean-Paul Sartre*. Kindhausen: Metanoia, 1996.

von Franz, Marie-Louise. *Alchemy: An Introduction to the Symbolism and Psychology*. Toronto: Inner City Books, 1980.

————. *Individuation in Fairy Tales*. Zurich: Spring, 1975.

————. *Projection and Re-Collection in Jungian Psychology.* William H. Kennedy, trans. La Salle, IL: Open Court, 1980.

Freud, S. *The Basic Writings of Sigmund Freud.* J. A. Brill, ed. New York: Modern Library/Random House, 1938.

Galegos, E. S. *The Personal Totem Pole.* Santa Fe, NM: Bear & Co., 1982.

The Gospel According to Thomas. A. Guillaumont, et al., trans. New York: Harper & Brothers, 1959.

Holy Bible: Containing Old and New Testaments. Authorized King James Version. London: Oxford University Press, n.d. See also: *The New English Bible: The New Testament.* Oxford: Oxford University Press, 1961.

Jacobi, Jolande. *The Way of Individuation.* New York: Harcourt Brace & World, 1967.

Jung, C. G. *Aion: Researches into the Phenomenology of the Self.* The Collected Works, vol. 9ii. Bollingen Series XX. R. F. C. Hull, trans. Princeton: Princeton University Press, 1969.

————. *Alchemical Studies.* The Collected Works, vol. 13. Bollingen Series XX. R. F. C. Hull, trans. Princeton: Princeton University Press, 1967.

————. *The Archetypes and the Collective Unconscious.* The Collected Works, vol. 9i. Bollingen Series XX. R. F. C. Hull, trans. Princeton: Princeton University Press, 1959.

————. *Civilization in Transition.* The Collected Works, vol. 10. Bollingen Series XX. R. F. C. Hull, trans. Princeton: Princeton University Press, 1964/1970.

—. *Man and His Symbols*. New York: Laurel/Dell, 1968.

—. *Memories, Dreams, Reflections*. Aniela Jaffe, ed. New York: Pantheon, 1963.

—. *Practice of Psychotherapy*. The Collected Works, vol. 16. Bollingen Series XX. R. F. C. Hull, trans. Princeton: Princeton University Press, 1954.

—. *Psychological Types*. The Collected Works, vol. 6. Bollingen Series XX. R. F. C. Hull, trans. Princeton: Princeton University Press, 1971.

—. *Psychology and Religion: West and East*. The Collected Works, vol. 11. Bollingen Series XX. R. F. C. Hull, trans. Princeton: Princeton University Press, 1958.

—. *The Psychology of Kundalini Yoga: Notes of a Seminar Given in 1932 by C. G. Jung*. Bollingen Series XCIX. Sonu Shamdasani, ed. Princeton: Princeton University Press, 1996.

—. *The Symbolic Life: Miscellaneous Writings*. The Collected Works, vol. 18. Bollingen Series XX. R. F. C. Hull, trans. Princeton: Princeton University Press, 1976.

—. *Two Essays on Analytical Psychology*. The Collected Works, vol. 7. Bollingen Series XX. R. F. C. Hull, trans. Princeton: Princeton University Press, 1953.

—. *The Visions Seminars*, 2 vols. From the Complete Notes of Mary Foote. Zurich: Spring, 1976.

———. "Psychological Commentary on Kundalini Yoga, Lectures One and Two (12 October and 19 October), 1932," in *Spring: An Annual of Archetypal Psychology and Jungian Thought*. New York and Zurich, 1975.

———. "Psychological Commentary on Kundalini Yoga, Lectures Three and Four (26 October and 2 November) 1932," in *Spring: An Annual of Archetypal Psychology and Jungian Thought*. New York and Zurich, 1976.

Jung, C. G. and Richard Wilhelm. *The Secret of the Golden Flower: A Chinese Book of Life*. London: Routledge & Kegan Paul, 1931.

Kelsey, M.T. *Caring*. New York: Paulist Press, 1988.

Leadbeater, C. W. *The Chakras*. Wheaton: Quest/Theosophical, 1973. Originally published in Madras, India by the Theosophical Publishing House, 1927.

Plato. *Apology*. In *The Great Dialogues of Plato*. Benjamin Jowett, trans. Chicago: Encyclopaedia Britannica, 1952.

Riedel, Ingrid. *Farben*. Stuttgart: Kreuz Verlag, 1983.

Rosenberg, A. *Engel und Daemonen*. Munich: Prestel Verlag, 1967.

Russiche Volksmaerchen. August van Loeis of Menar, trans. Dusseldorf/Koln: Eugen Diederichs Verlag, 1959.

Salman, D. H. "La Regression au Service du Moi dans l'Experience religieuse," in *Archiv fuer Religionspsychologie*, vol. 9. Paris, 1967.

Schellenbaum, P. *Wir Sehen uns im Andern*. Kindhausen: Metanoia, 1986.

Shelmerdine, Susan C., ed. *Homeric Hymns*. Newburyport, MA: Focus Publishing/R. Pullins Co., Inc., 1995.

Wallimann, S. *Umpolung*. Freiburg: Bauer Verlag, 1988.